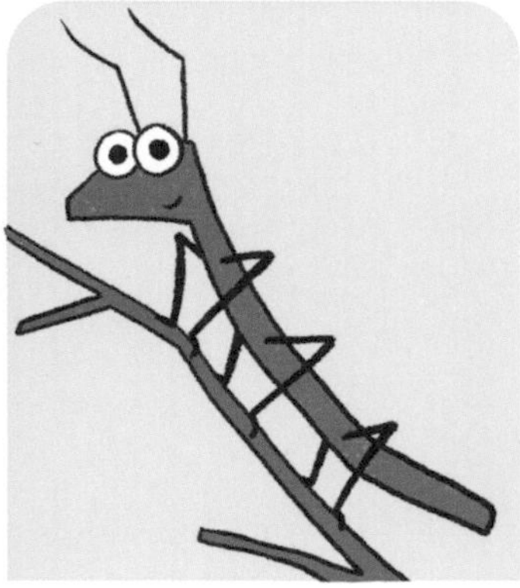

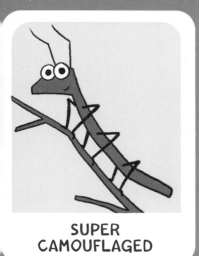

SUPER CAMOUFLAGED

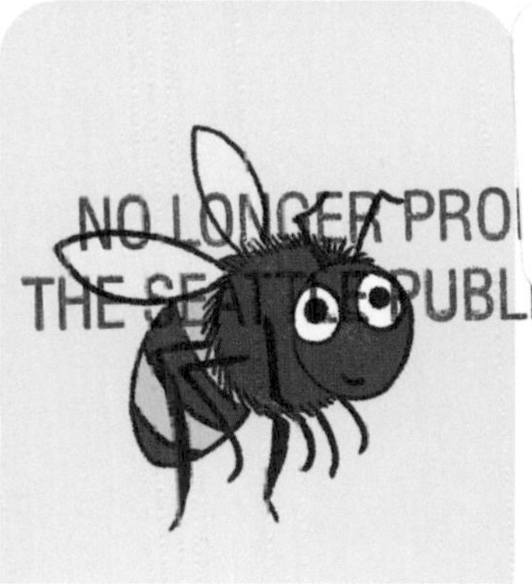

SUPER HARD WORKER

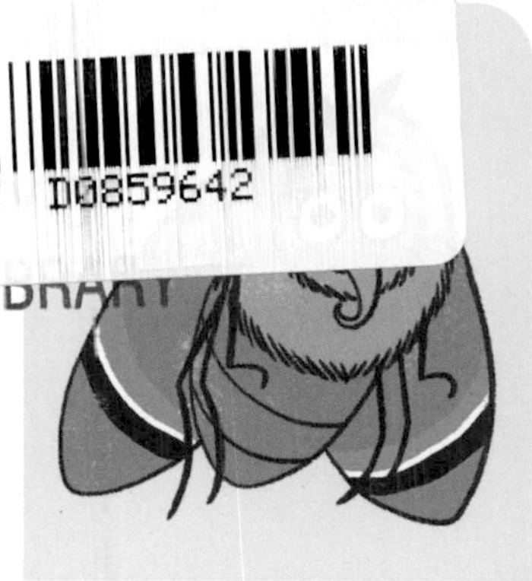

SUPER ULTRASONIC BLASTER

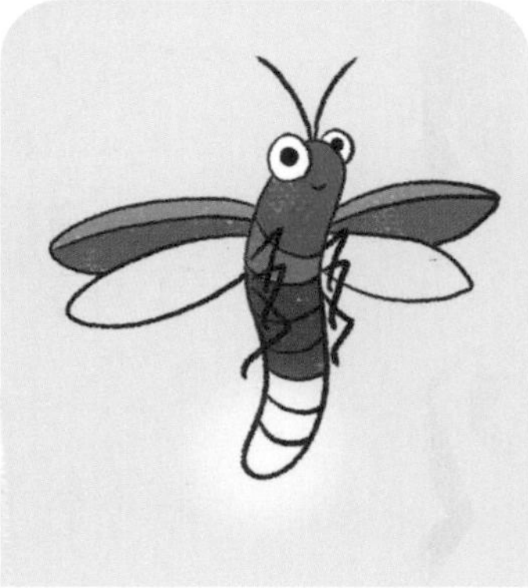

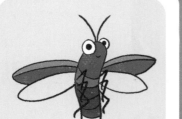

SUPER BRIGHT BUM

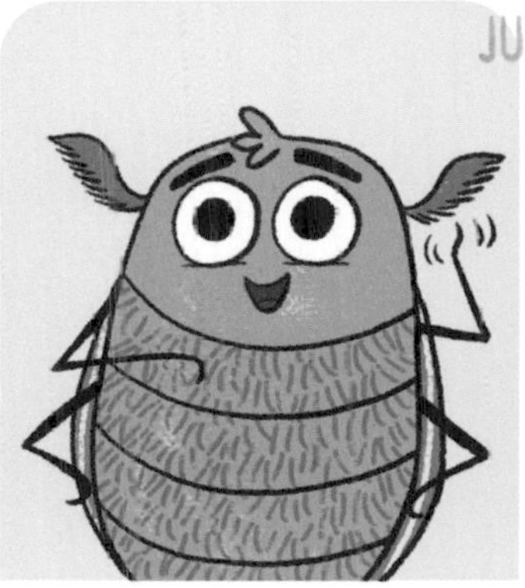

SUPER HAPPY TO BE HERE

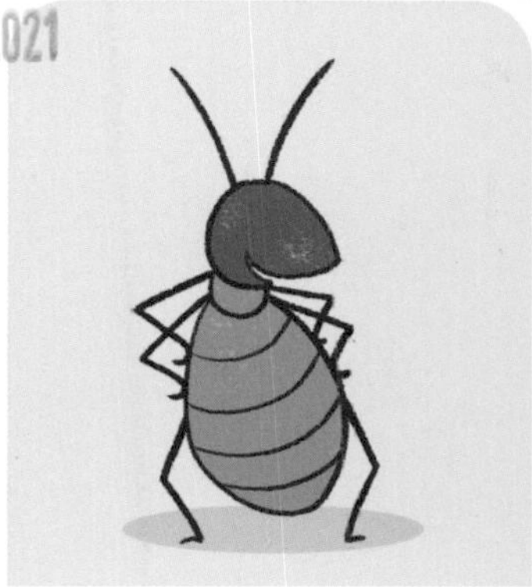

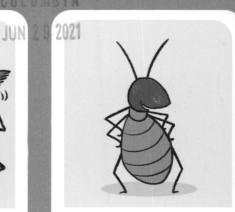

SUPER VENOM SPRAYER

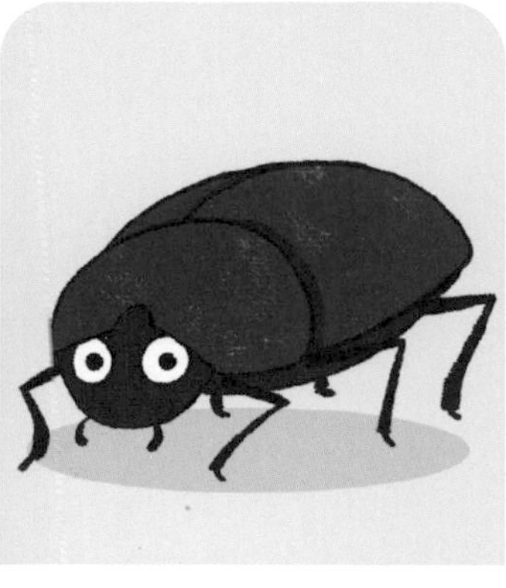

SUPER EXCITED ABOUT POOP

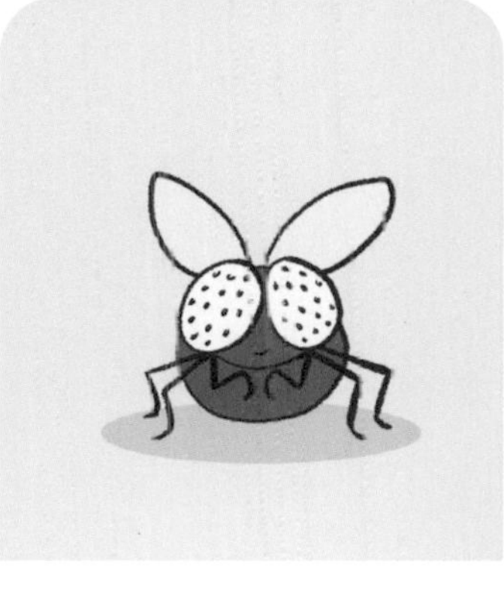

SUPER SIGHT

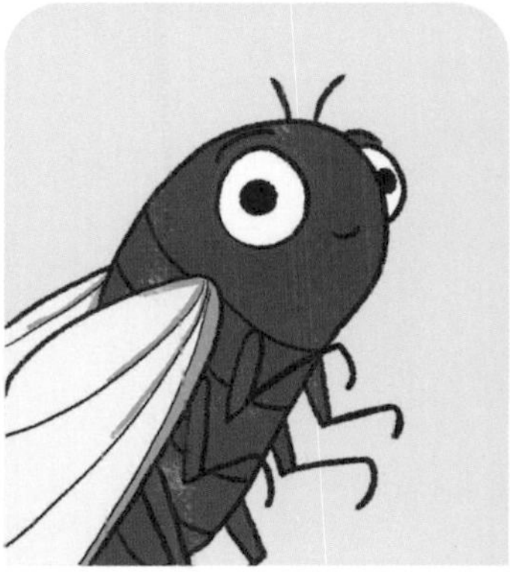

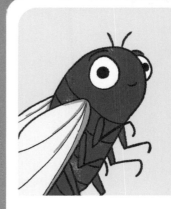

SUPER NOISY

Ashley Spires

BURT THE BEETLE

DOESN'T BITE!

Because that's NOT
how you make friends!

KIDS CAN PRESS

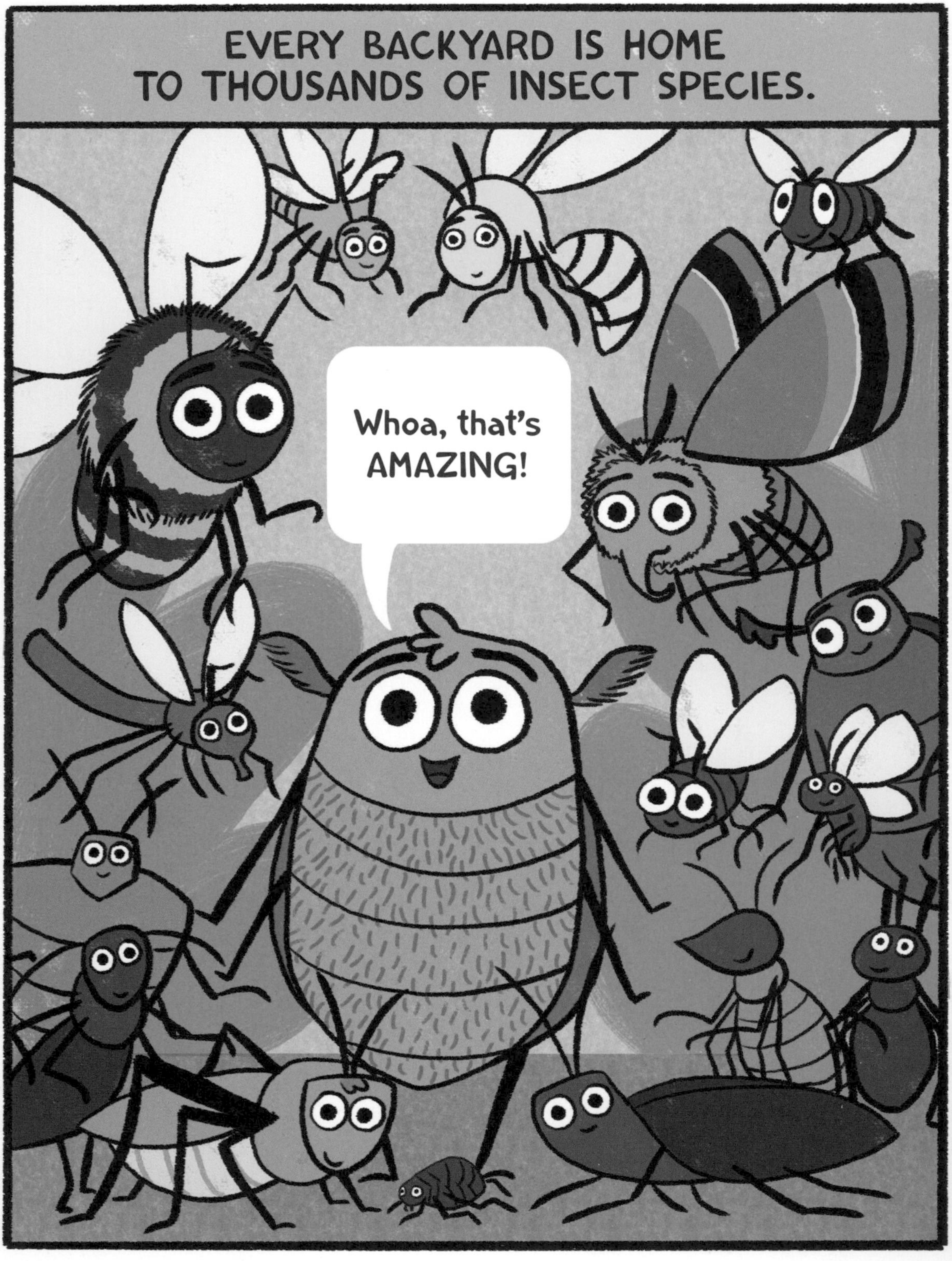
EVERY BACKYARD IS HOME TO THOUSANDS OF INSECT SPECIES.
Whoa, that's AMAZING!

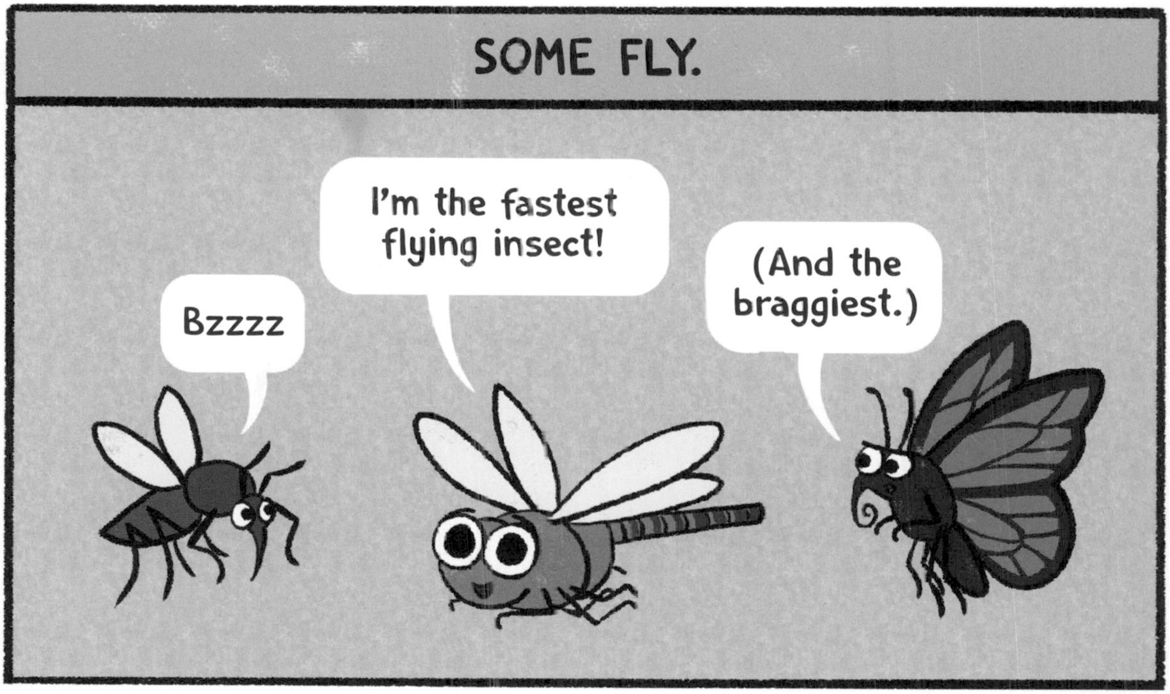
SOME FLY.
Bzzzz
I'm the fastest flying insect!
(And the braggiest.)

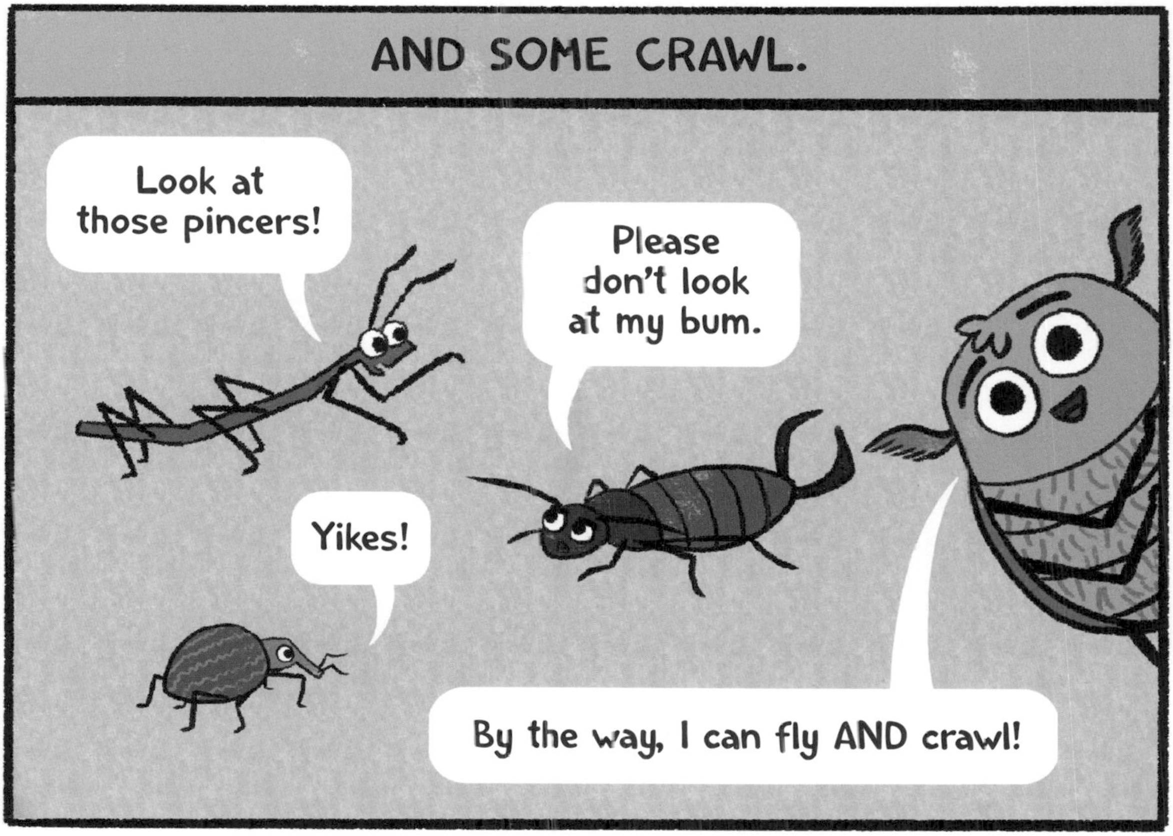
AND SOME CRAWL.
Look at those pincers!
Please don't look at my bum.
Yikes!
By the way, I can fly AND crawl!

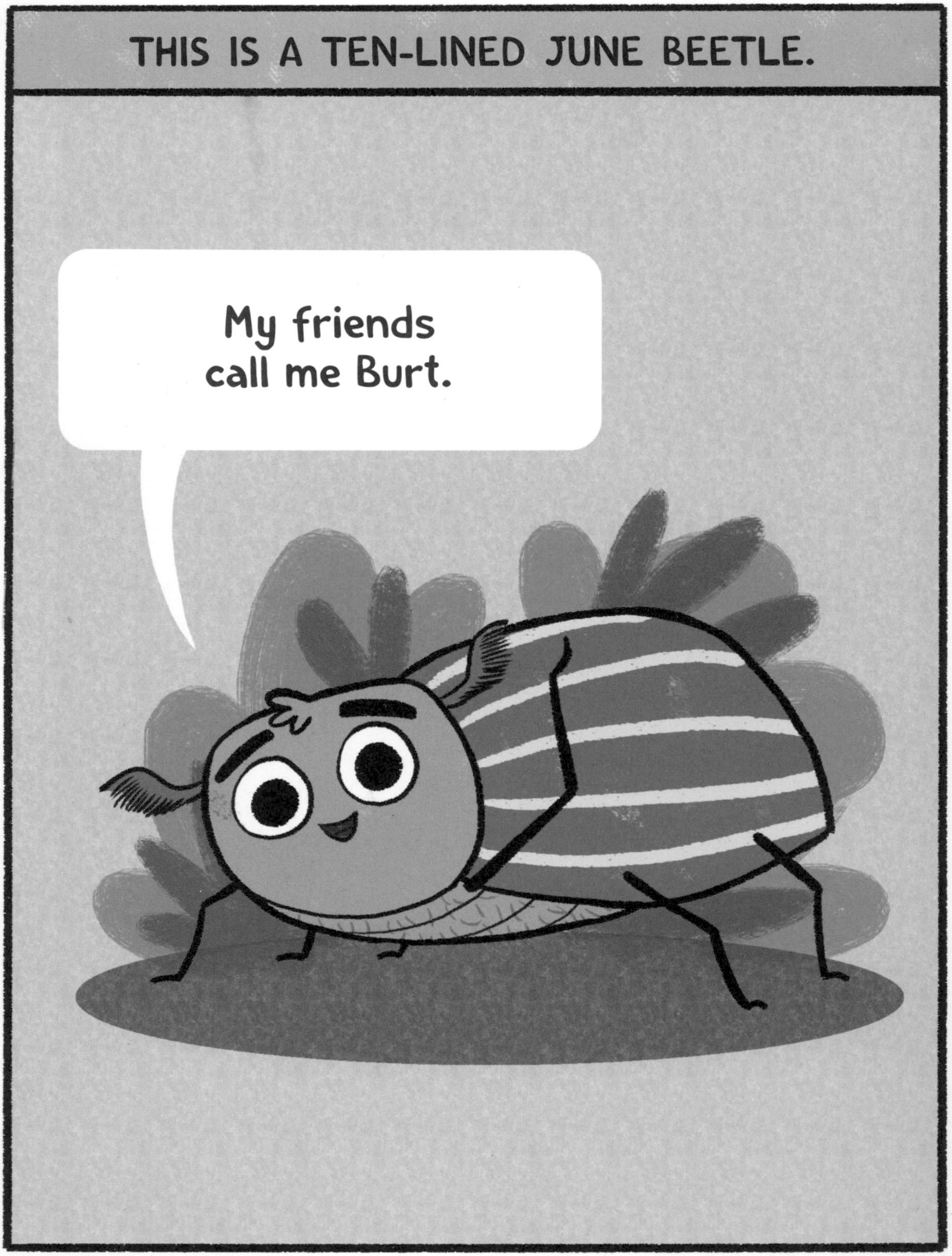
THIS IS A TEN-LINED JUNE BEETLE.
My friends call me Burt.

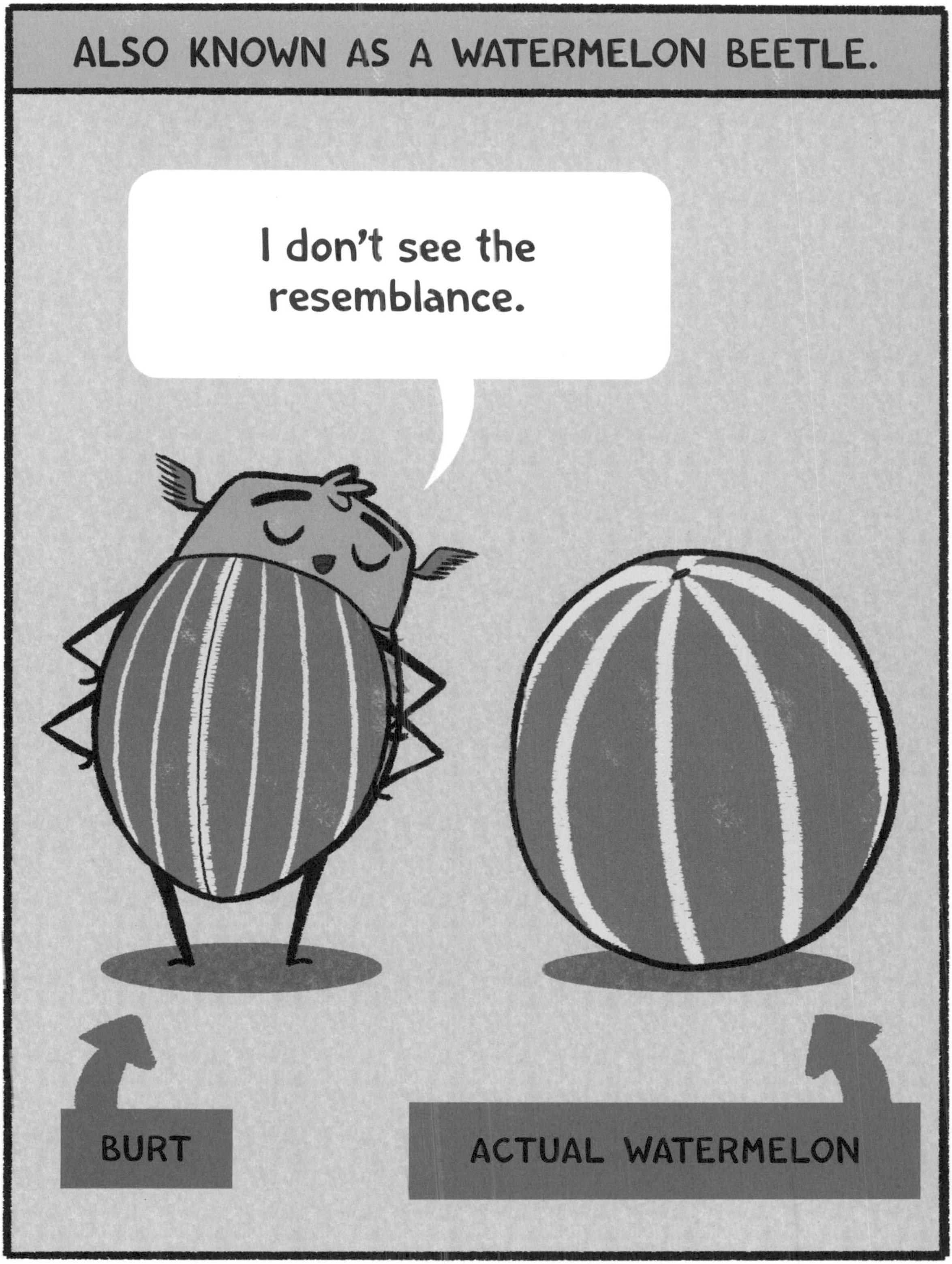
ALSO KNOWN AS A WATERMELON BEETLE.
I don't see the resemblance.
BURT
ACTUAL WATERMELON

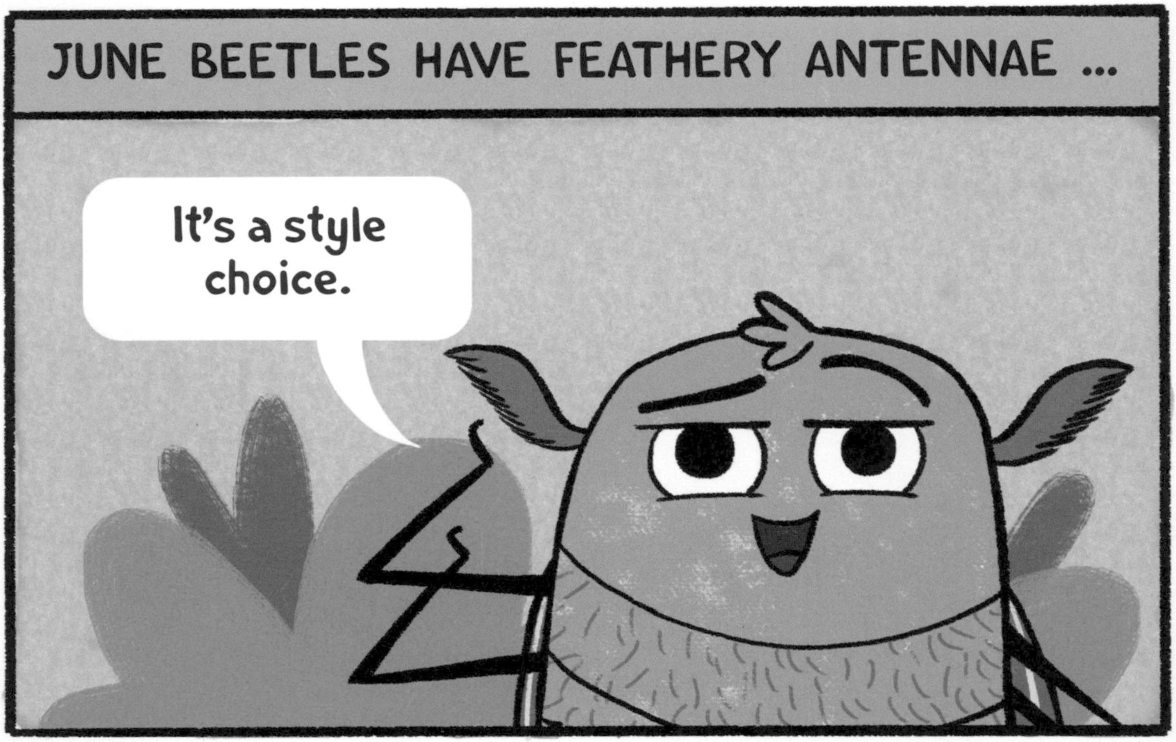
JUNE BEETLES HAVE FEATHERY ANTENNAE ...
It's a style choice.

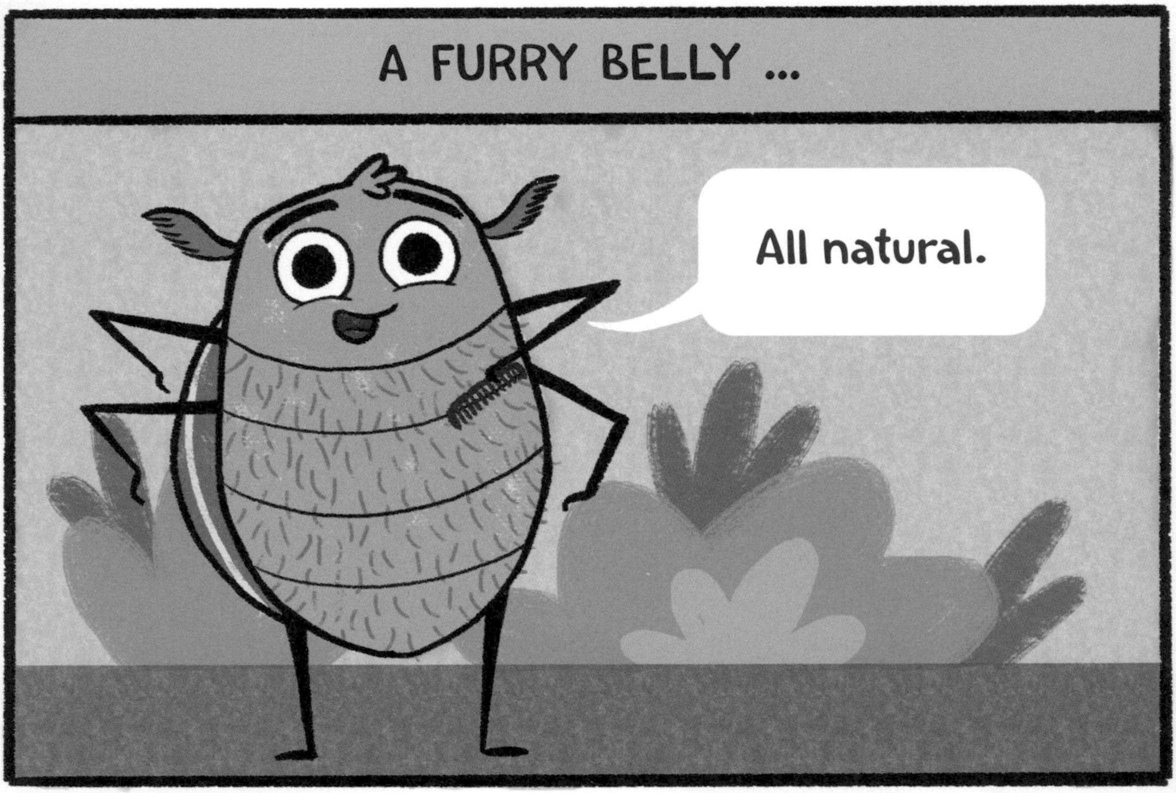
A FURRY BELLY ...
All natural.

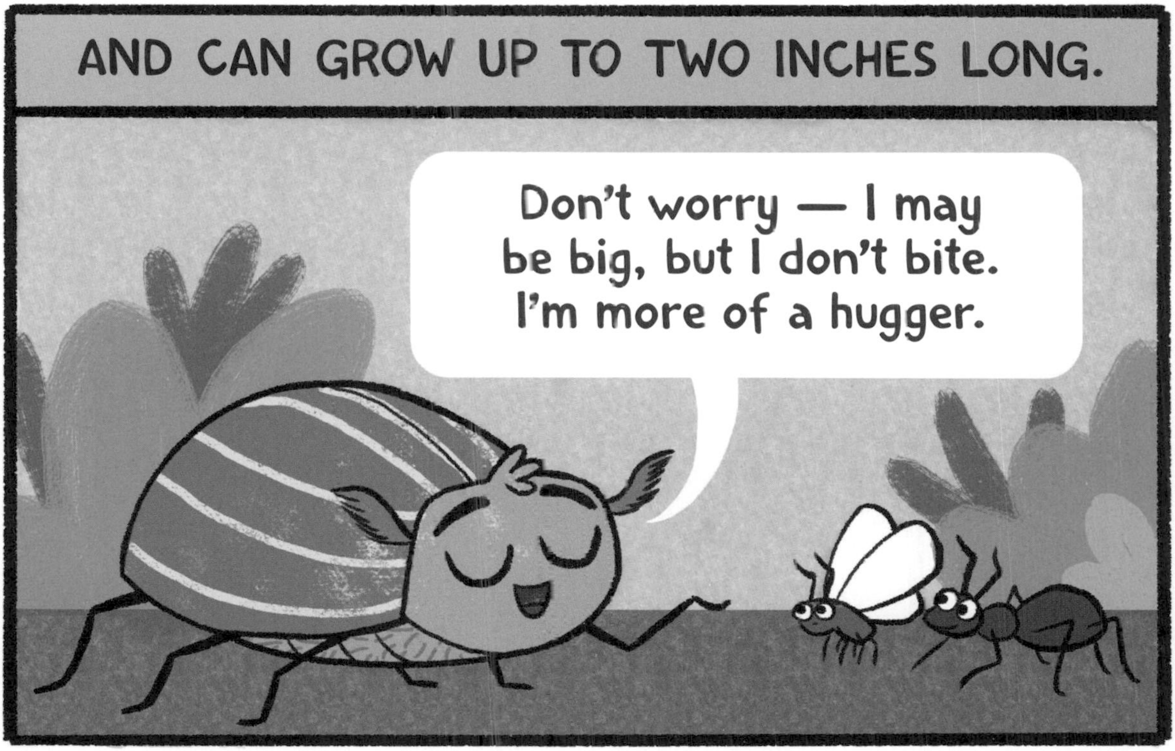
AND CAN GROW UP TO TWO INCHES LONG.
Don't worry — I may be big, but I don't bite. I'm more of a hugger.

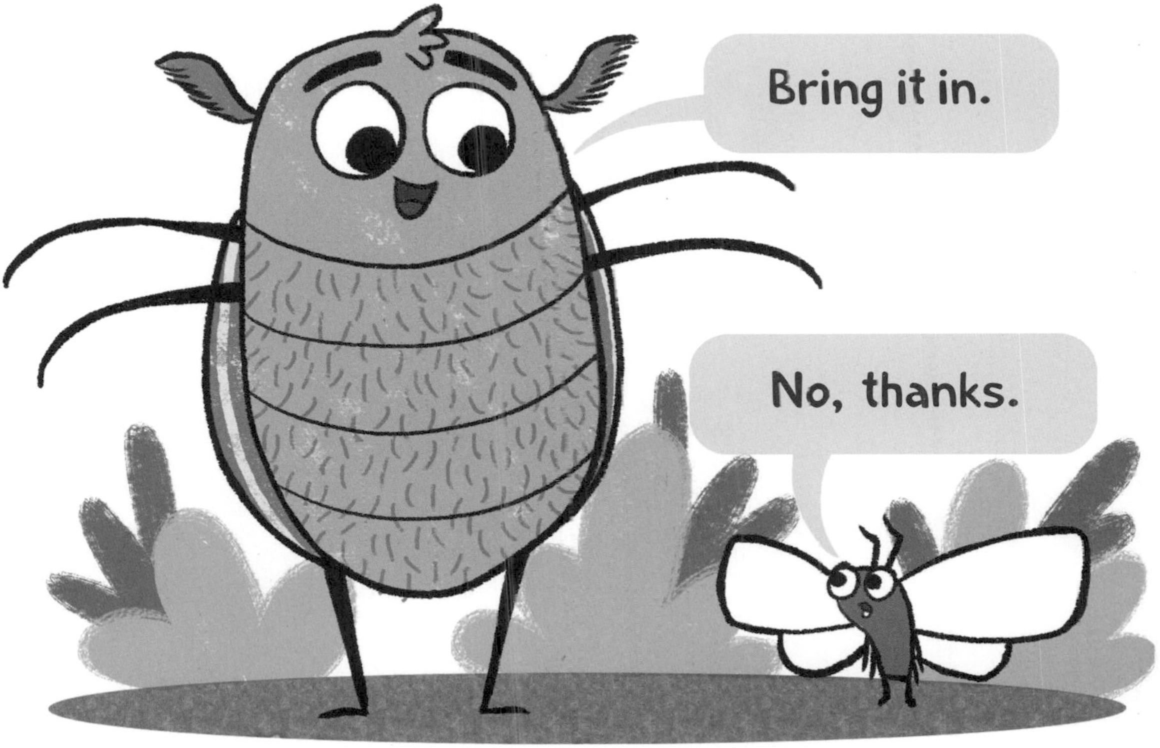
Bring it in.
No, thanks.

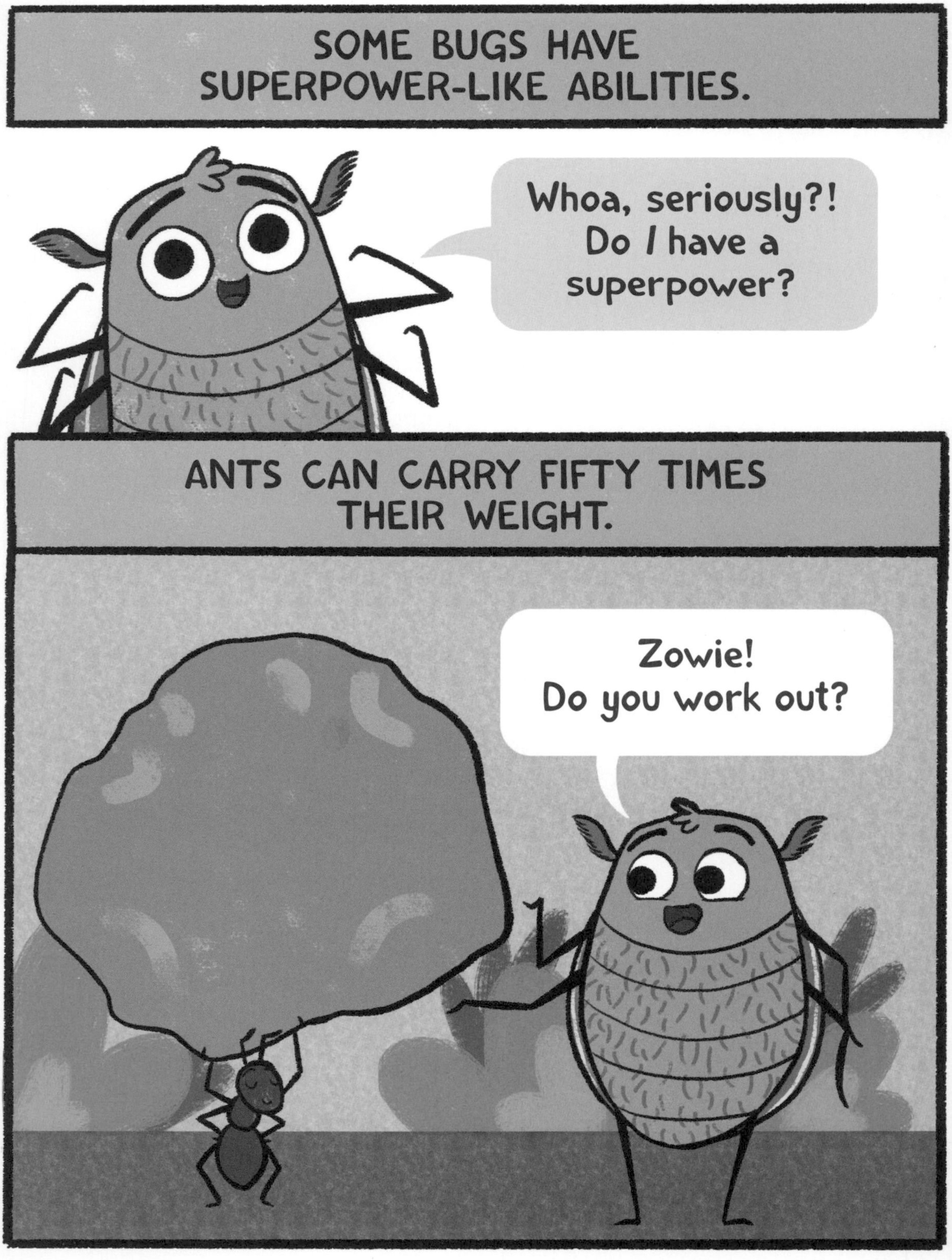
SOME BUGS HAVE SUPERPOWER-LIKE ABILITIES.
Whoa, seriously?! Do *I* have a superpower?
ANTS CAN CARRY FIFTY TIMES THEIR WEIGHT.
Zowie! Do you work out?

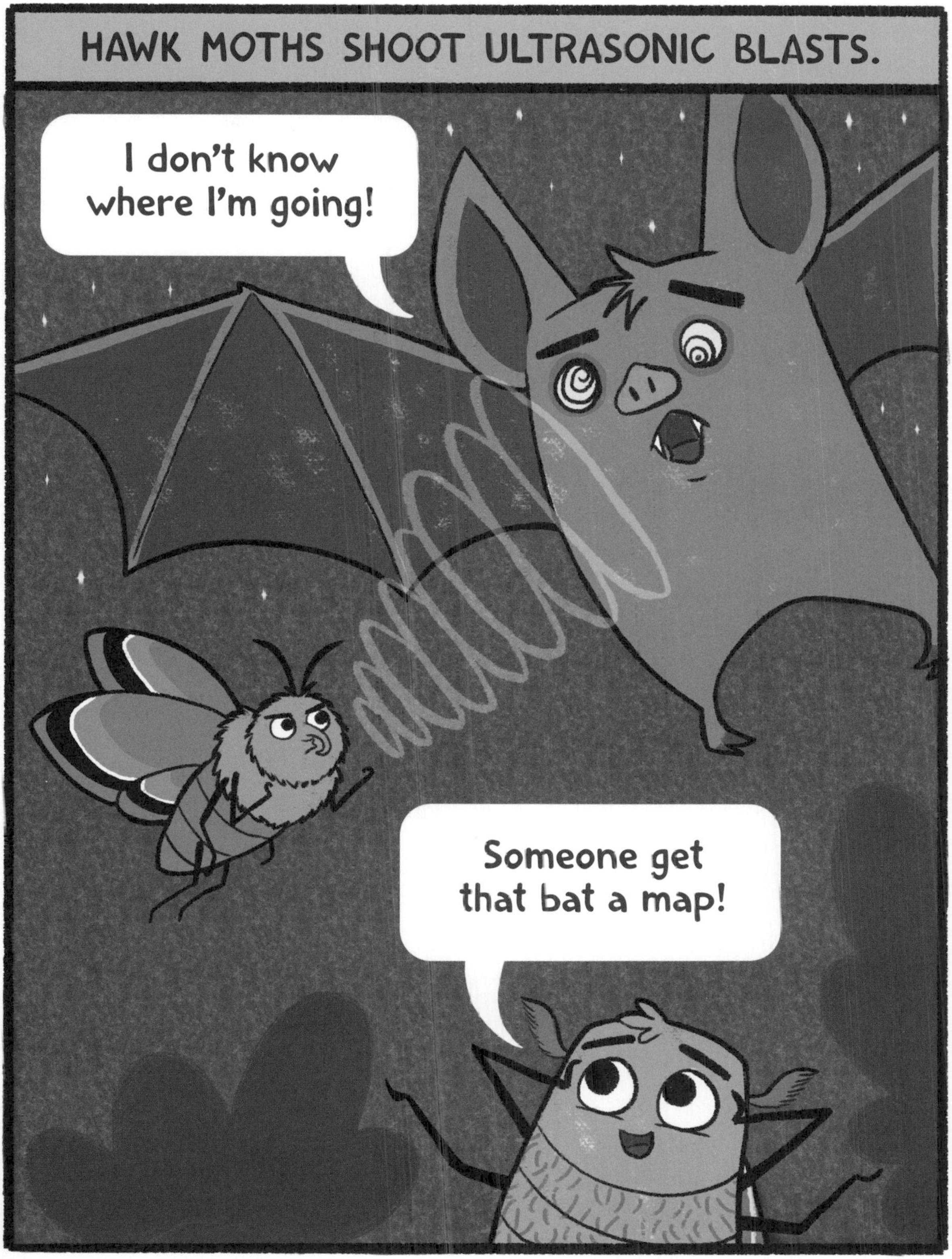
HAWK MOTHS SHOOT ULTRASONIC BLASTS.
I don't know where I'm going!
Someone get that bat a map!

SOME TERMITES CAN SPRAY PARALYZING VENOM.

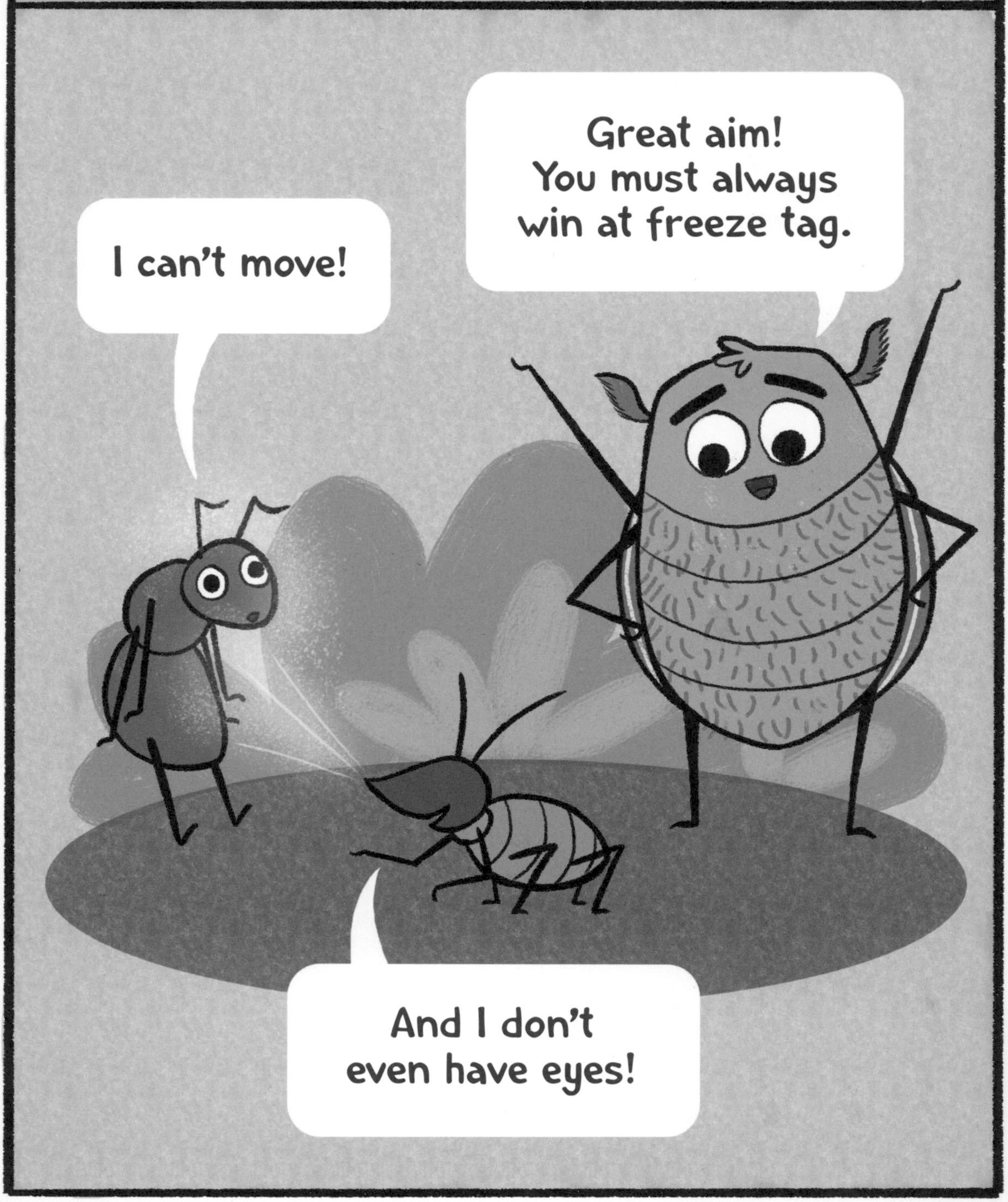

I can't move!
Great aim! You must always win at freeze tag.
And I don't even have eyes!

STINK BUGS RELEASE A BAD SMELL TO REPEL PREDATORS.

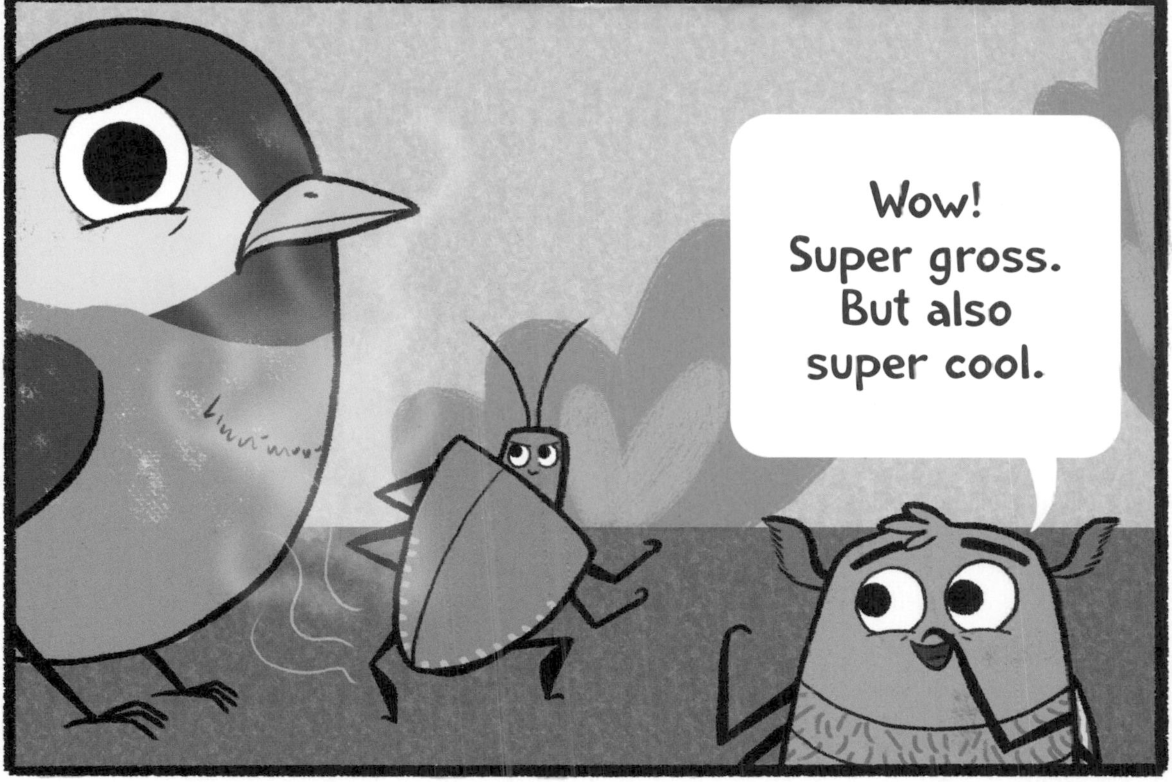
Wow! Super gross. But also super cool.

AND JUNE BEETLES ...

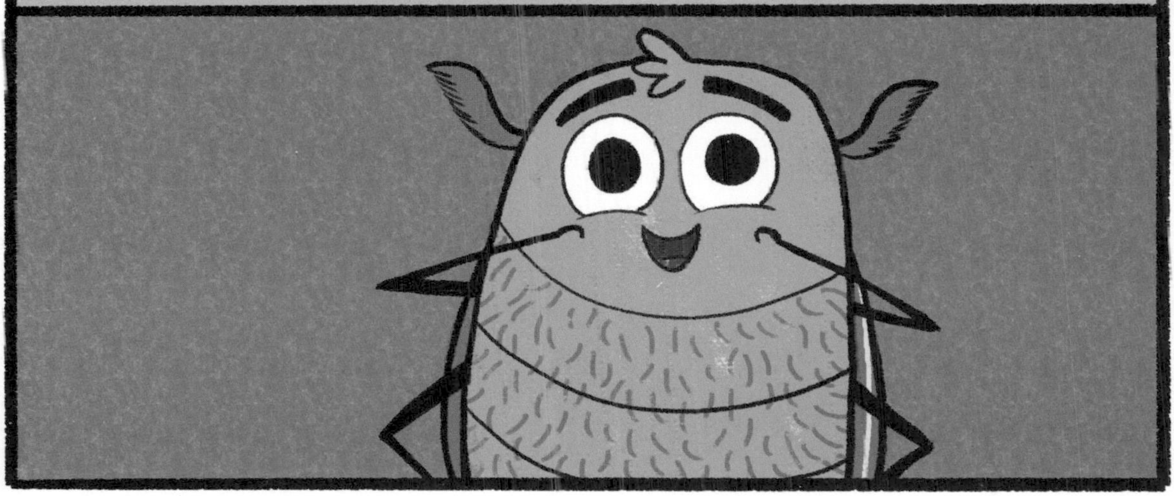

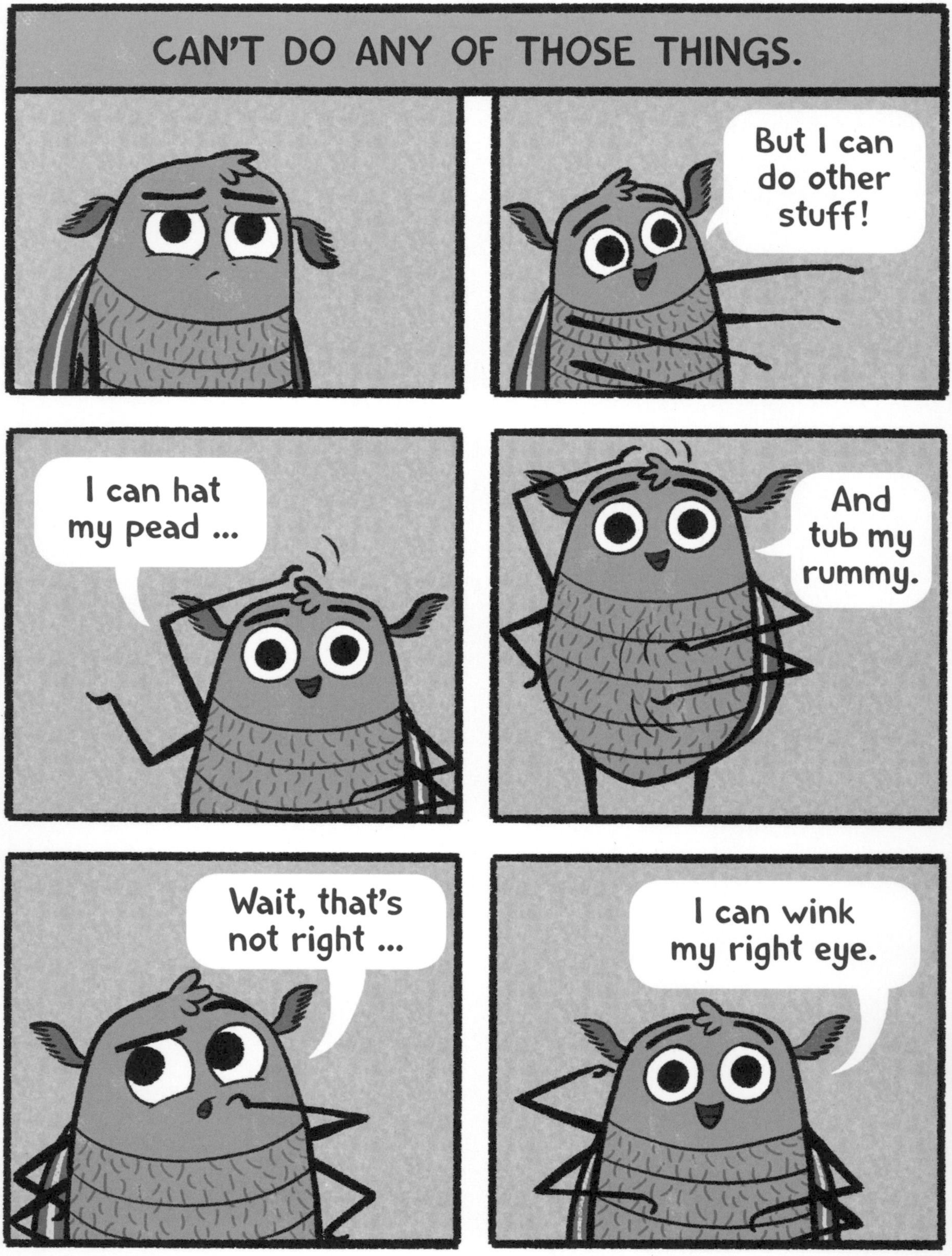
CAN'T DO ANY OF THOSE THINGS.
But I can do other stuff!
I can hat my pead ...
And tub my rummy.
Wait, that's not right ...
I can wink my right eye.

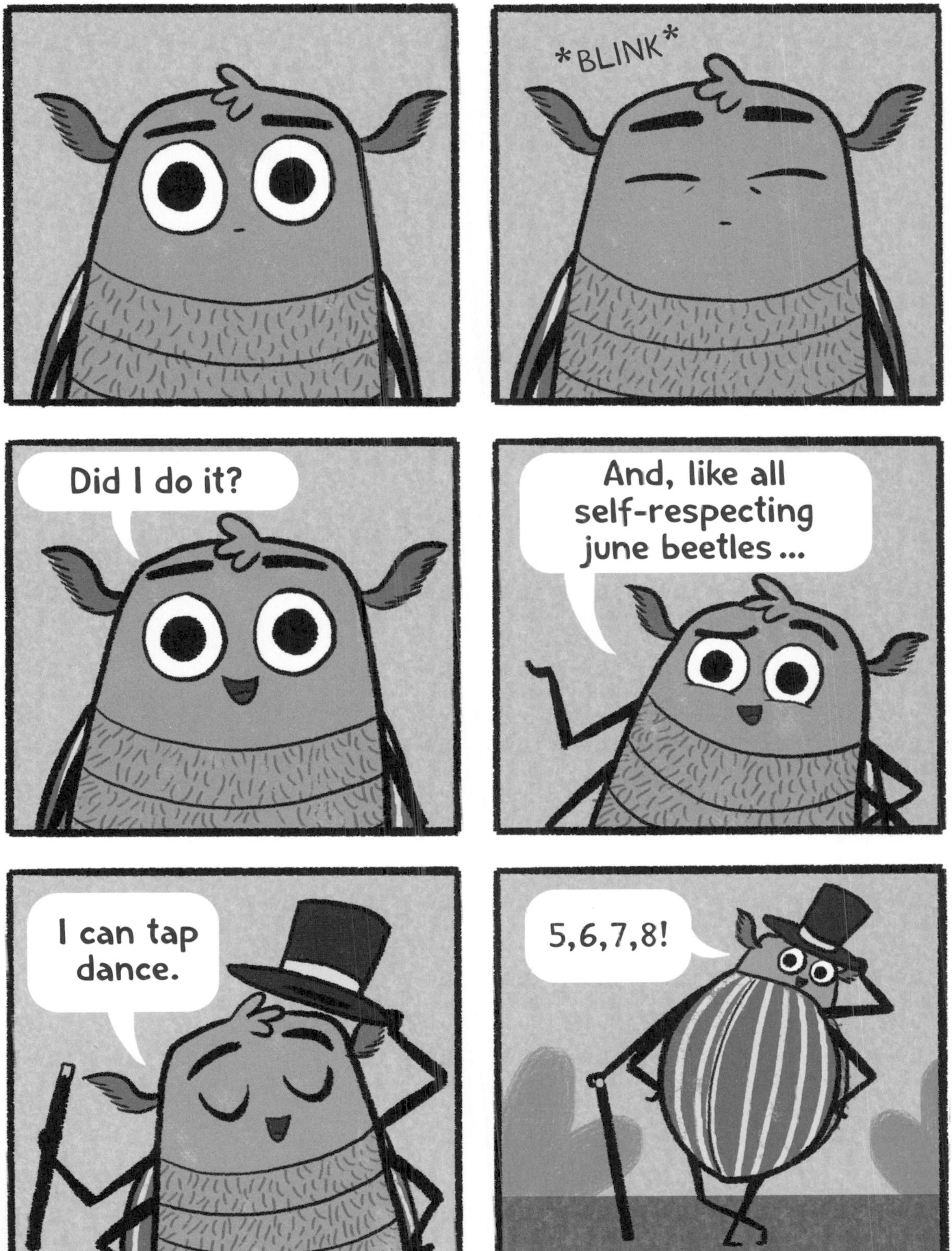
BLINK
Did I do it?
And, like all self-respecting june beetles ...
I can tap dance.
5,6,7,8!

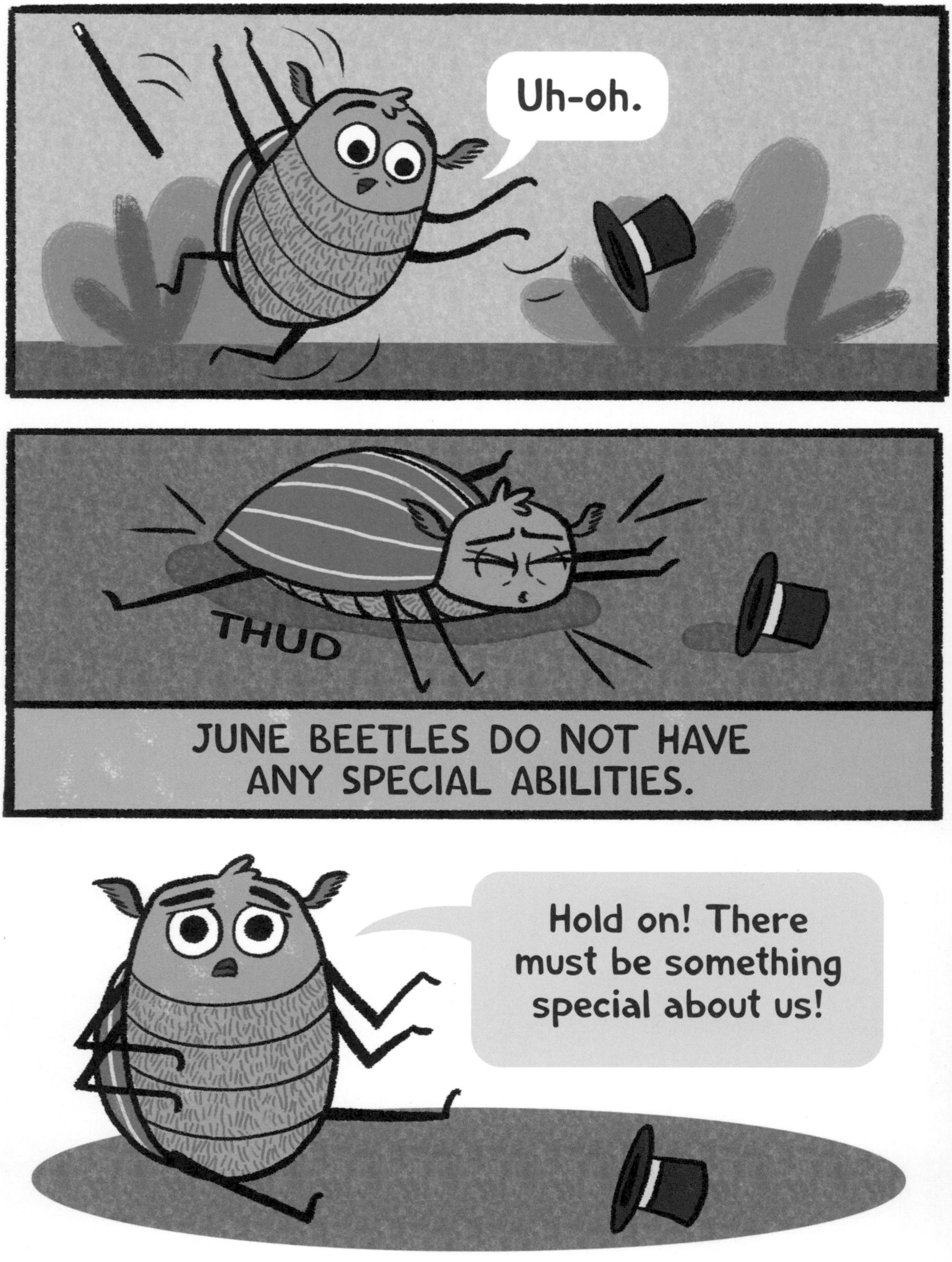
Uh-oh.
THUD
JUNE BEETLES DO NOT HAVE ANY SPECIAL ABILITIES.
Hold on! There must be something special about us!

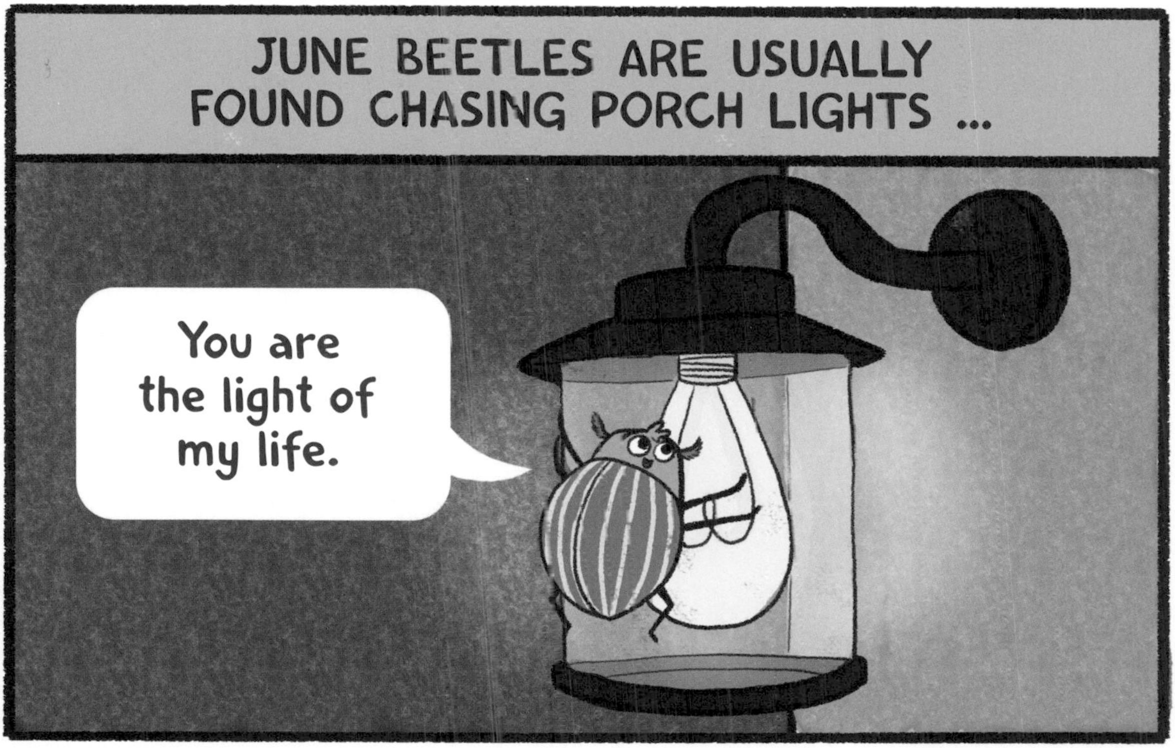
JUNE BEETLES ARE USUALLY FOUND CHASING PORCH LIGHTS ...
You are the light of my life.

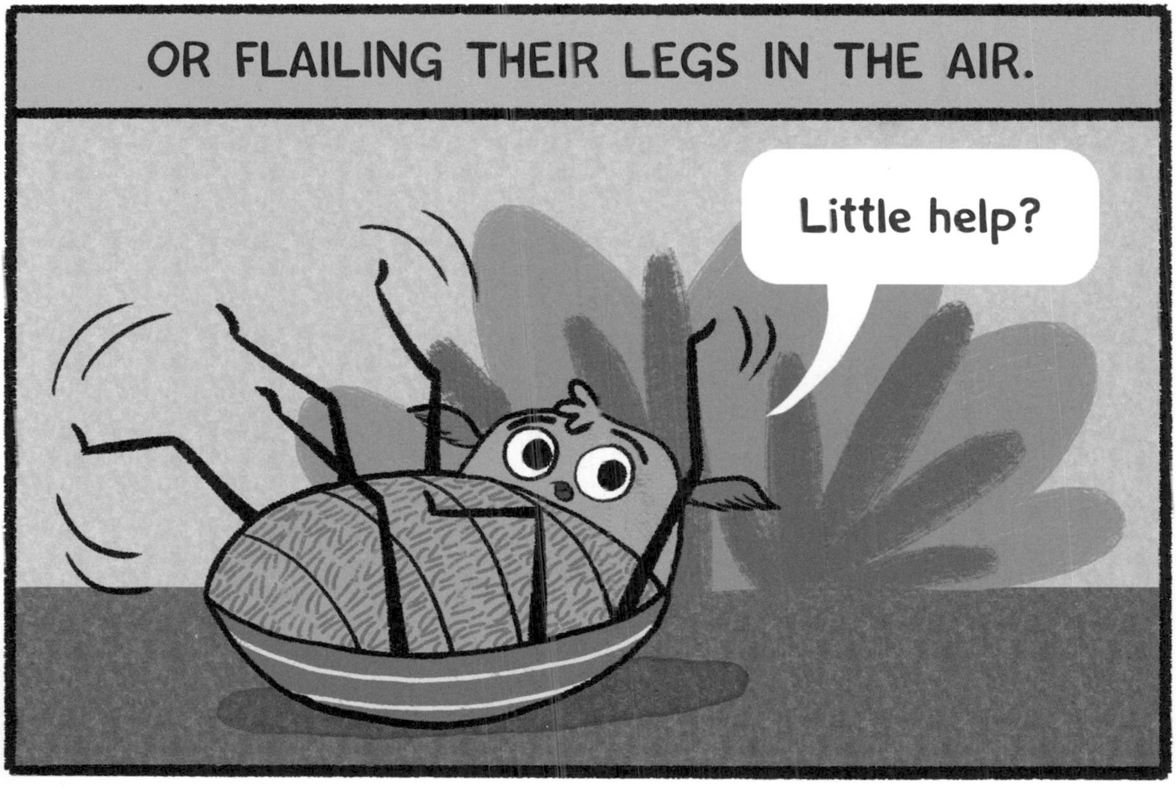
OR FLAILING THEIR LEGS IN THE AIR.
Little help?

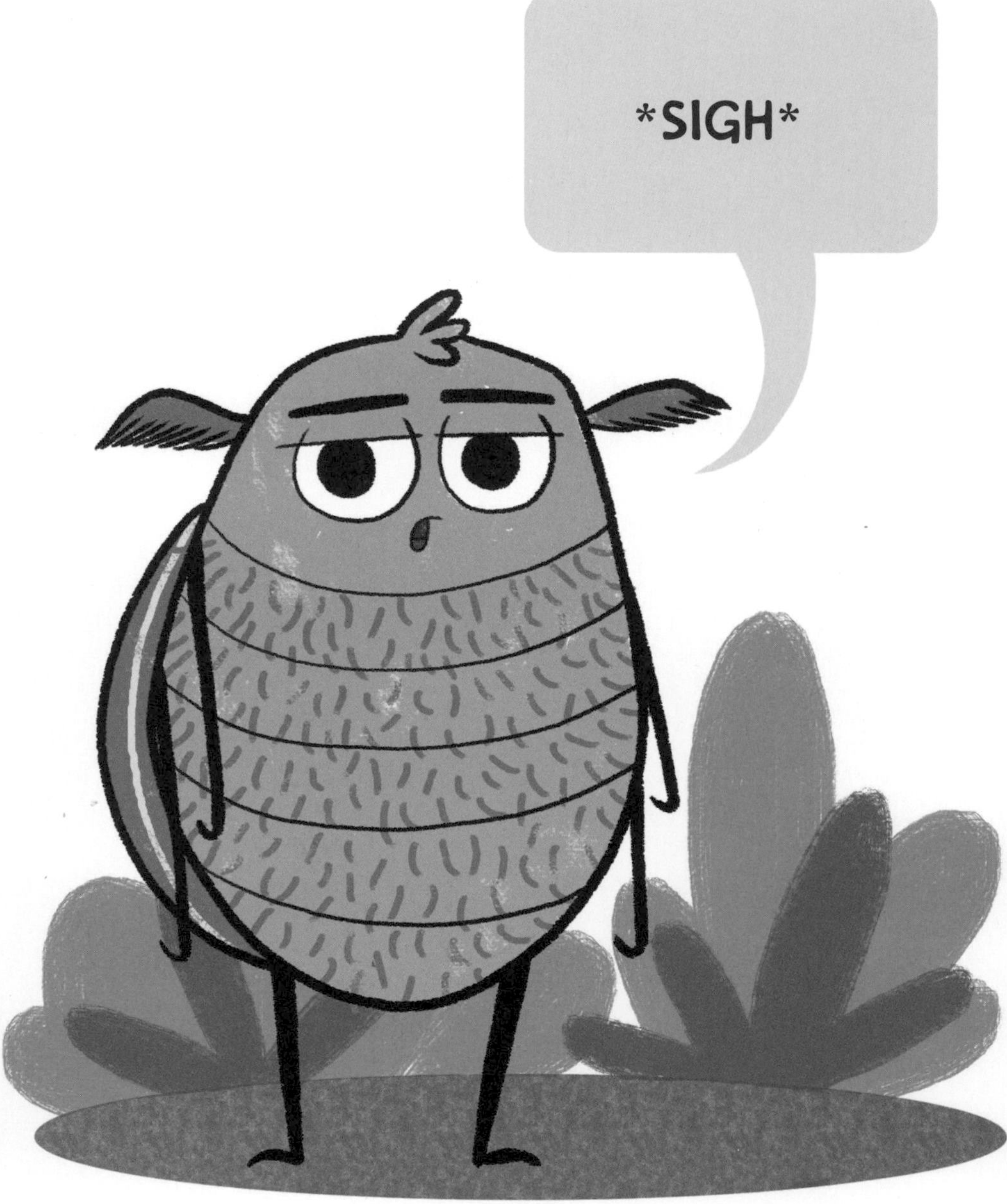
SIGH

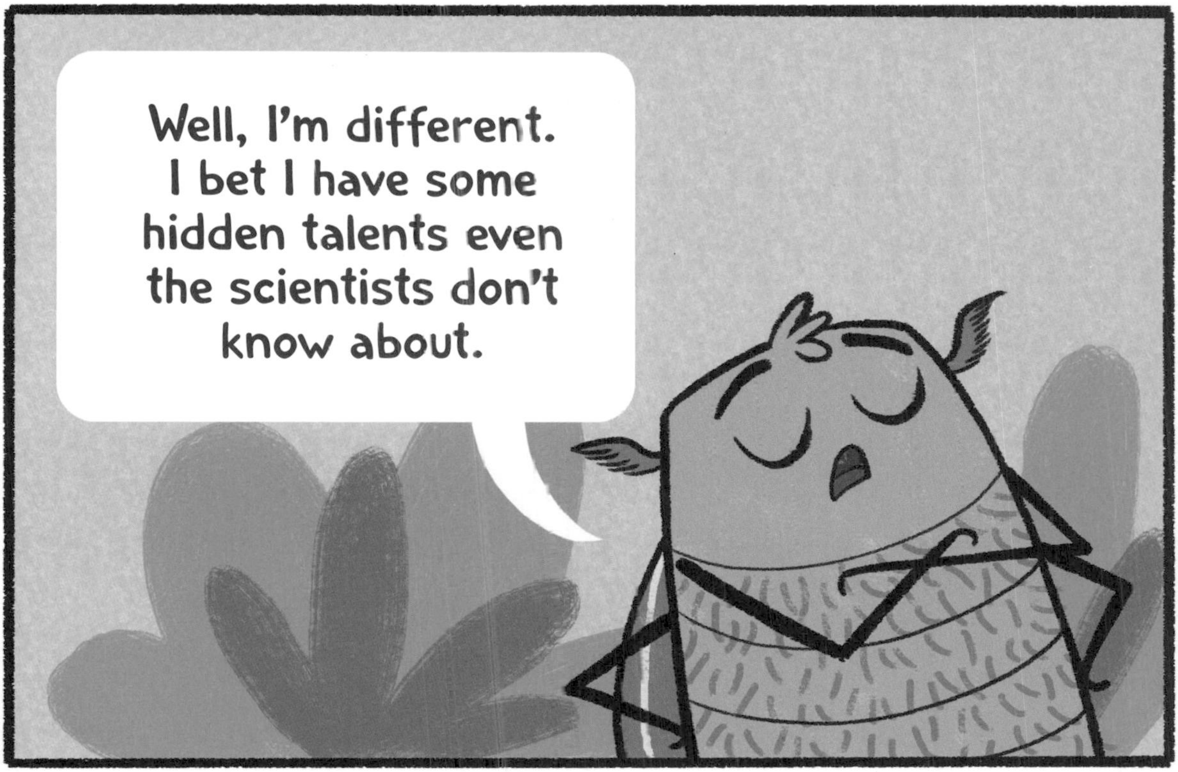
Well, I'm different. I bet I have some hidden talents even the scientists don't know about.

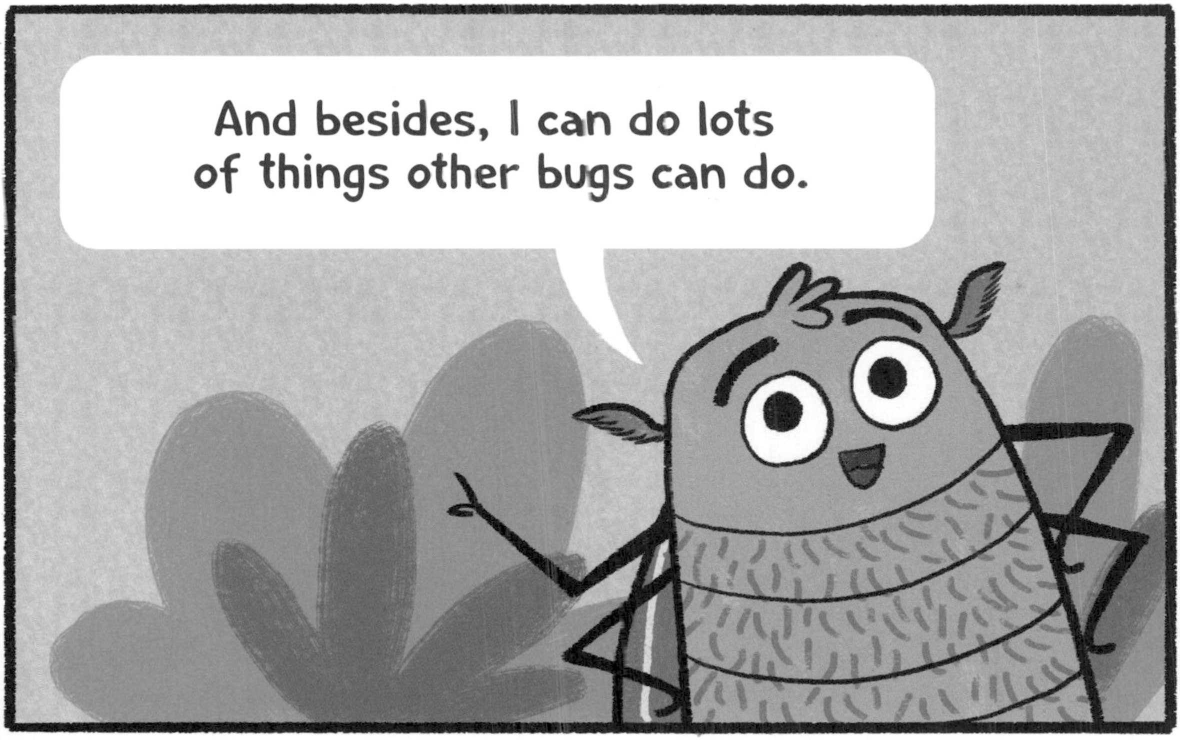
And besides, I can do lots of things other bugs can do.

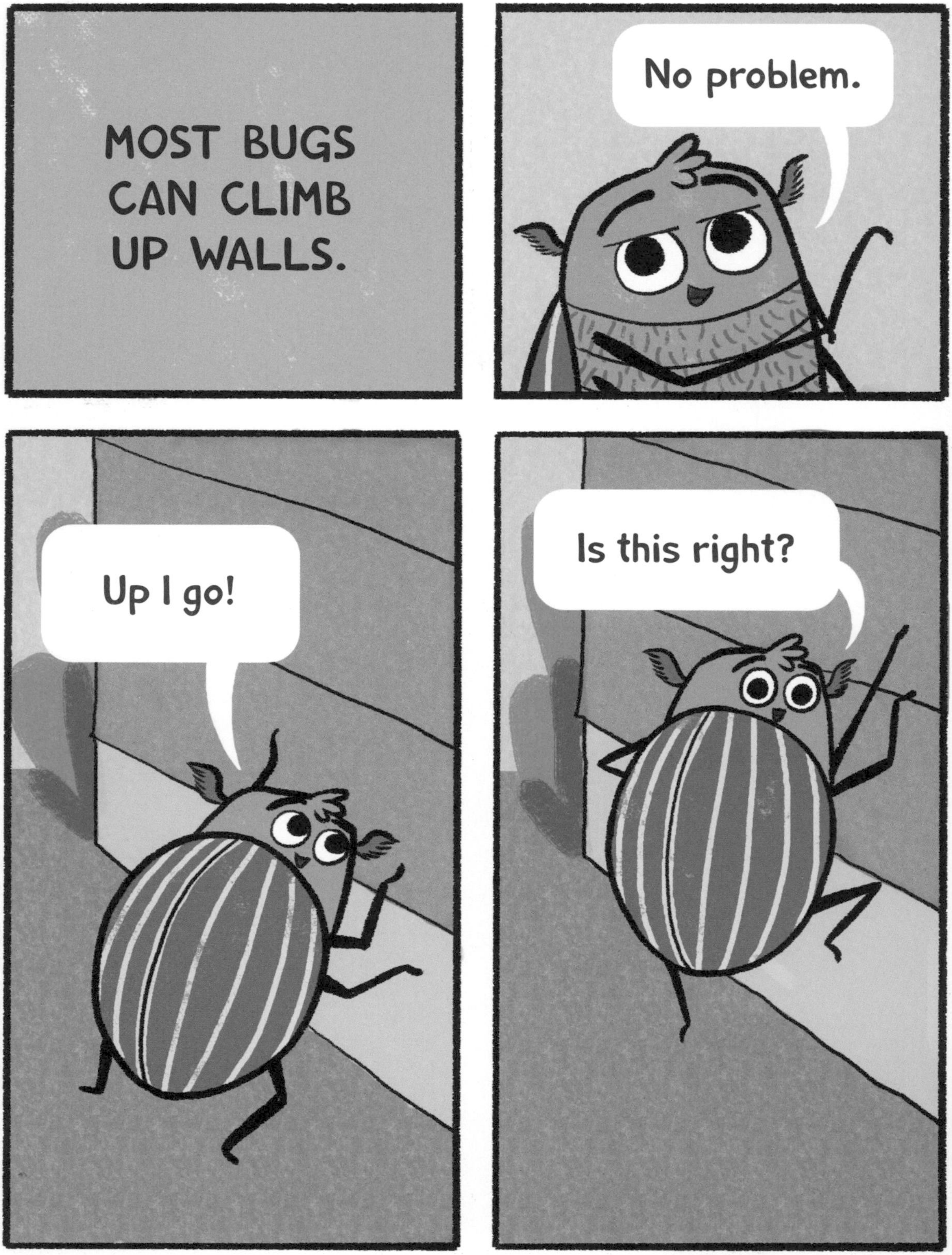
MOST BUGS CAN CLIMB UP WALLS.
No problem.
Up I go!
Is this right?

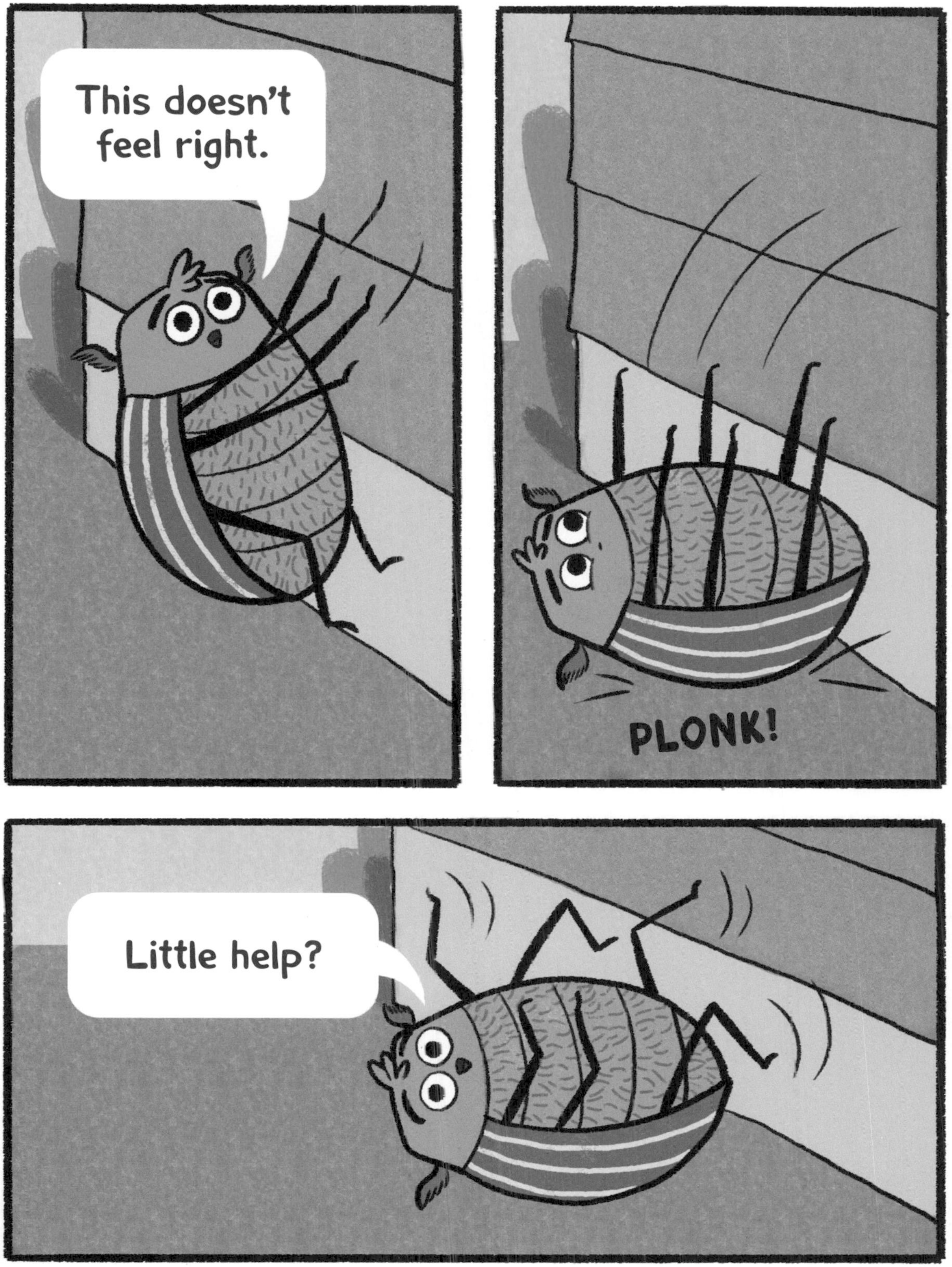
This doesn't feel right.
PLONK!
Little help?

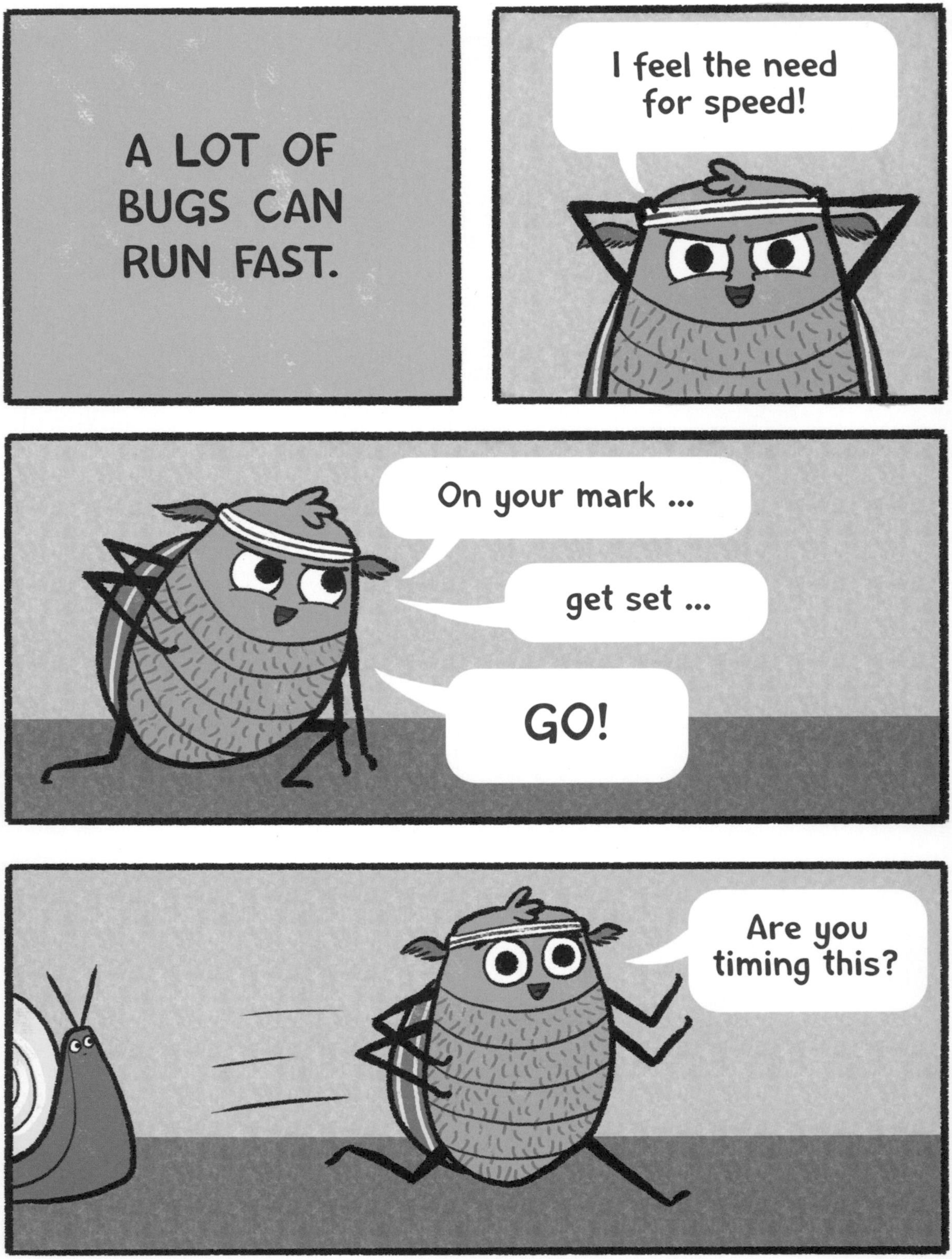
A LOT OF BUGS CAN RUN FAST.
I feel the need for speed!
On your mark ...
get set ...
GO!
Are you timing this?

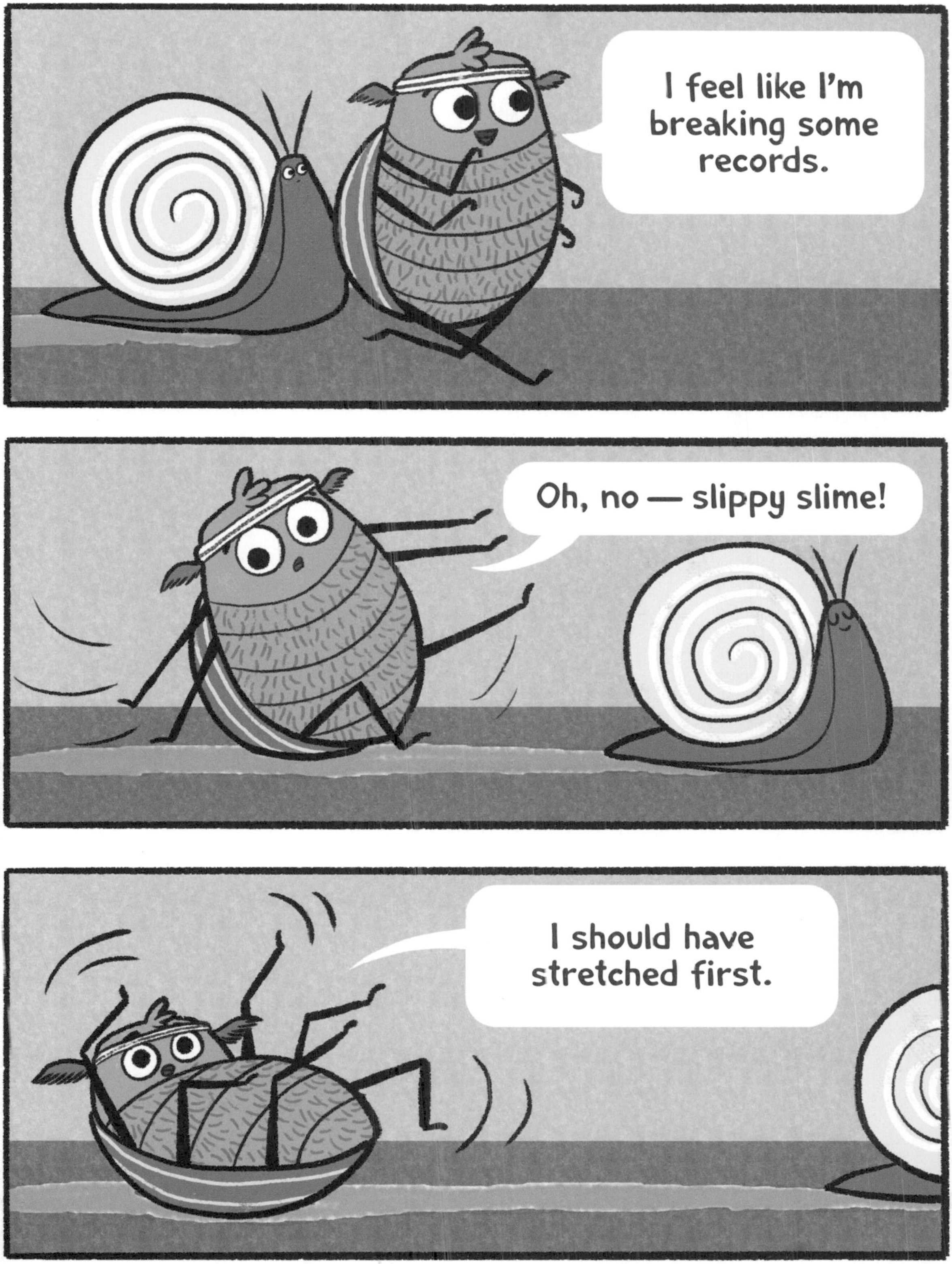
I feel like I'm breaking some records.
Oh, no — slippy slime!
I should have stretched first.

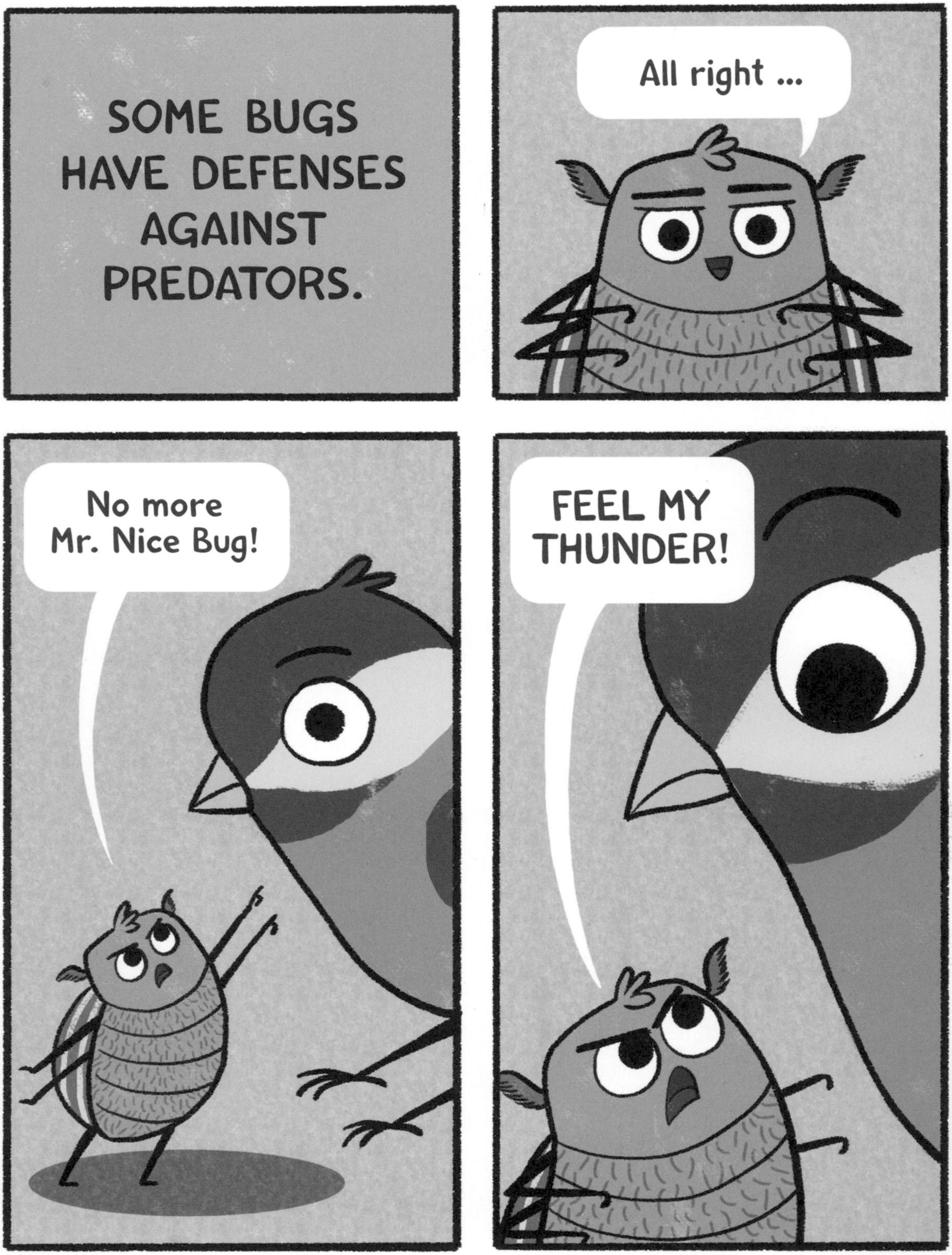
SOME BUGS HAVE DEFENSES AGAINST PREDATORS.
All right ...
No more Mr. Nice Bug!
FEEL MY THUNDER!

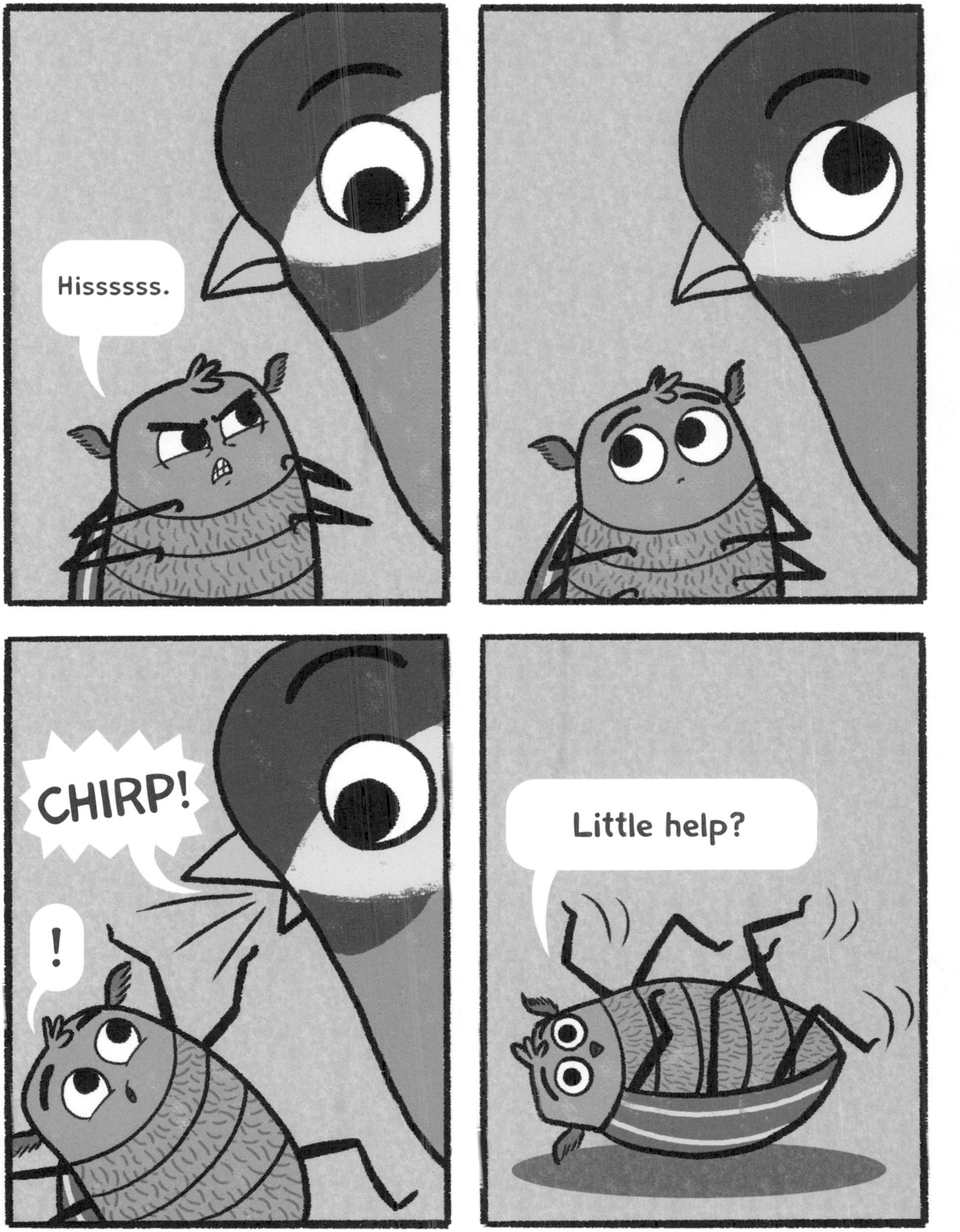
Hissssss.
CHIRP!
!
Little help?

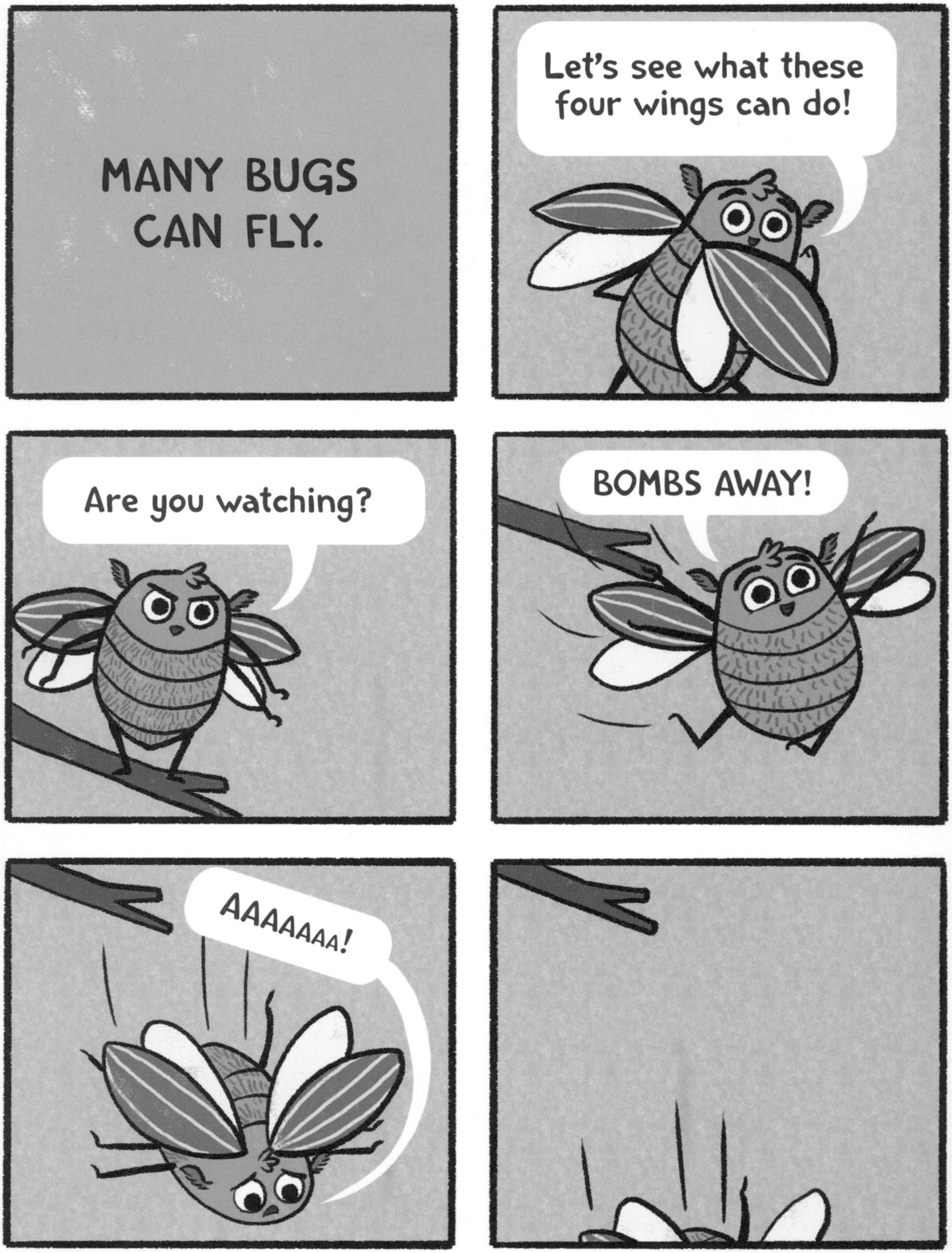
MANY BUGS CAN FLY.
Let's see what these four wings can do!
Are you watching?
BOMBS AWAY!
AAAAAAA!

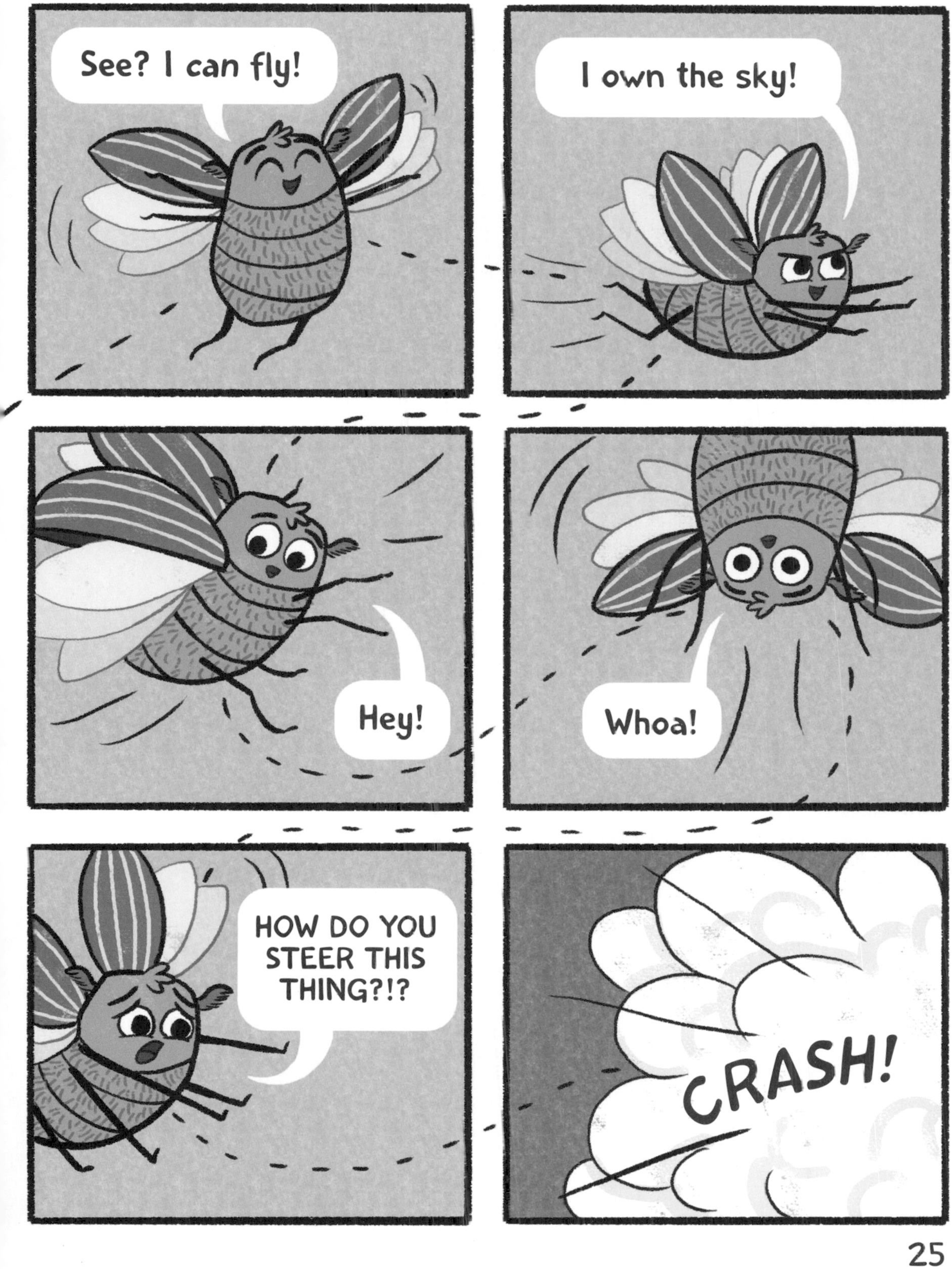
See? I can fly!
I own the sky!
Hey!
Whoa!
HOW DO YOU STEER THIS THING?!?
CRASH!

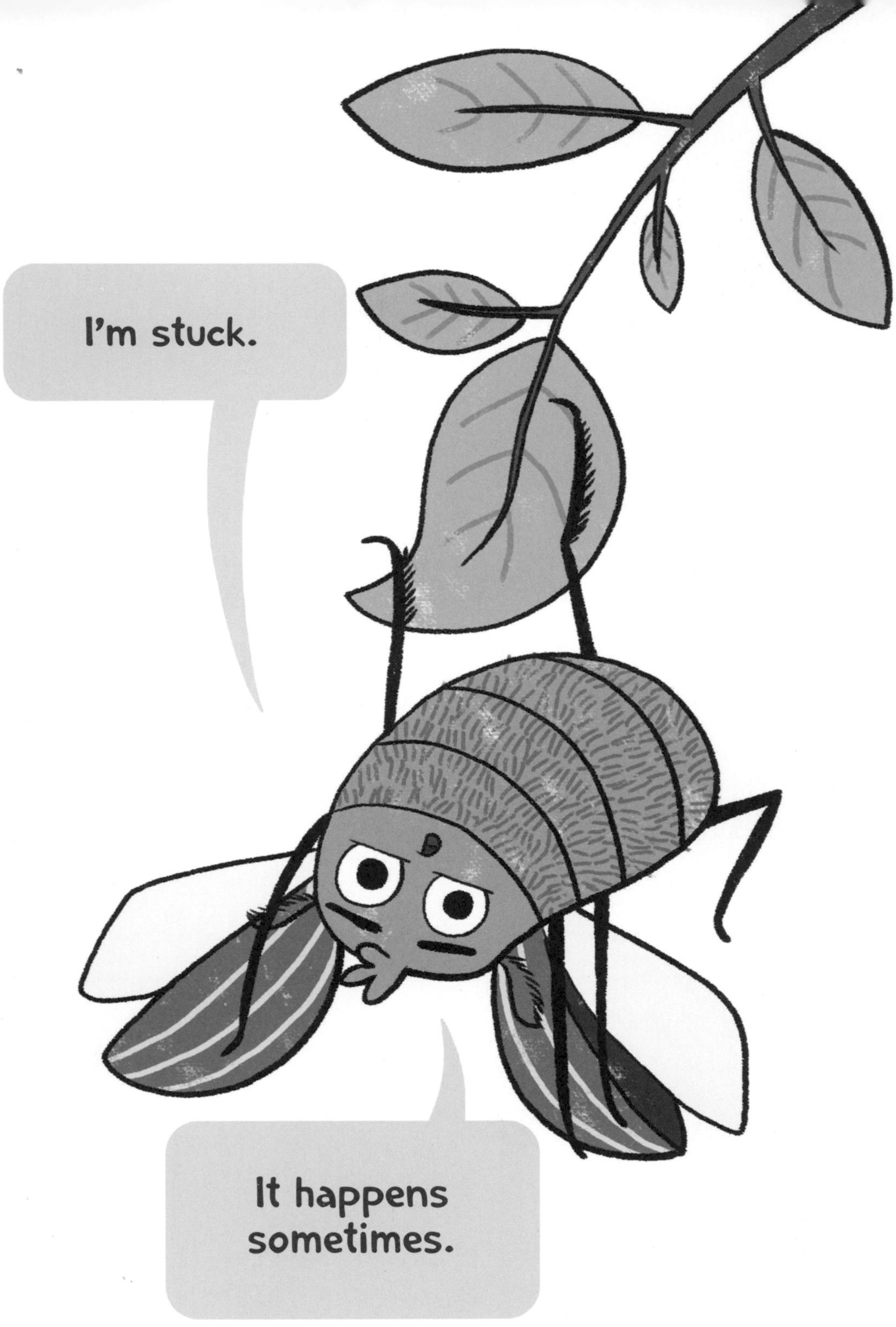
I'm stuck.
It happens sometimes.

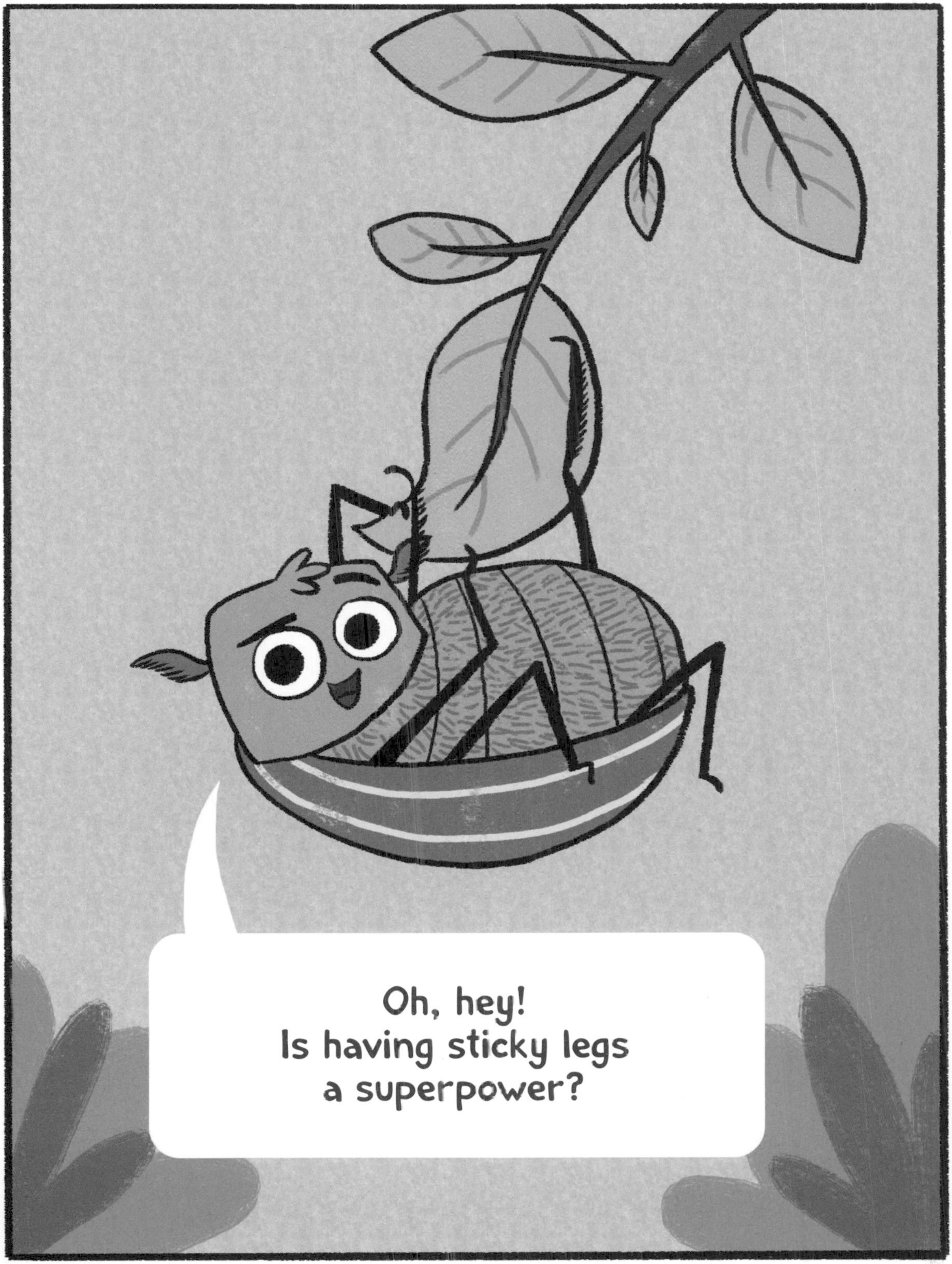
Oh, hey!
Is having sticky legs
a superpower?

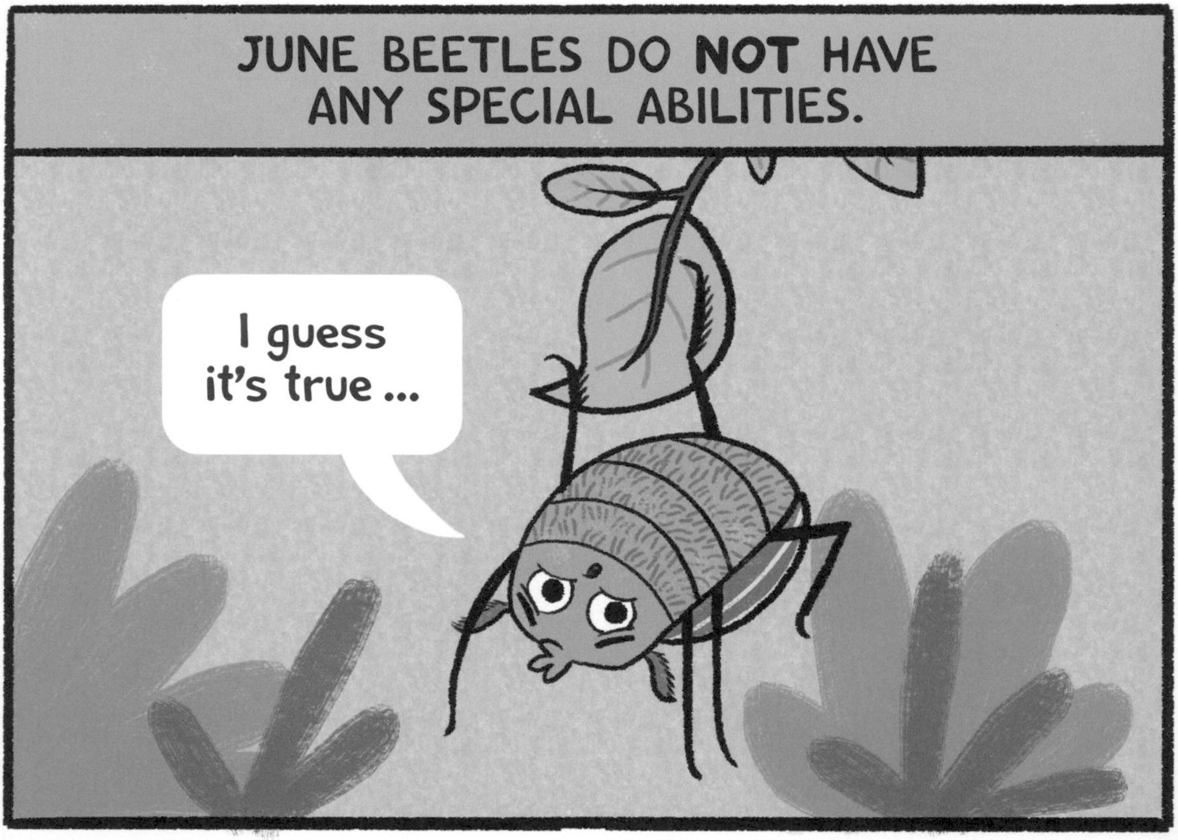
JUNE BEETLES DO **NOT** HAVE ANY SPECIAL ABILITIES.
I guess it's true ...

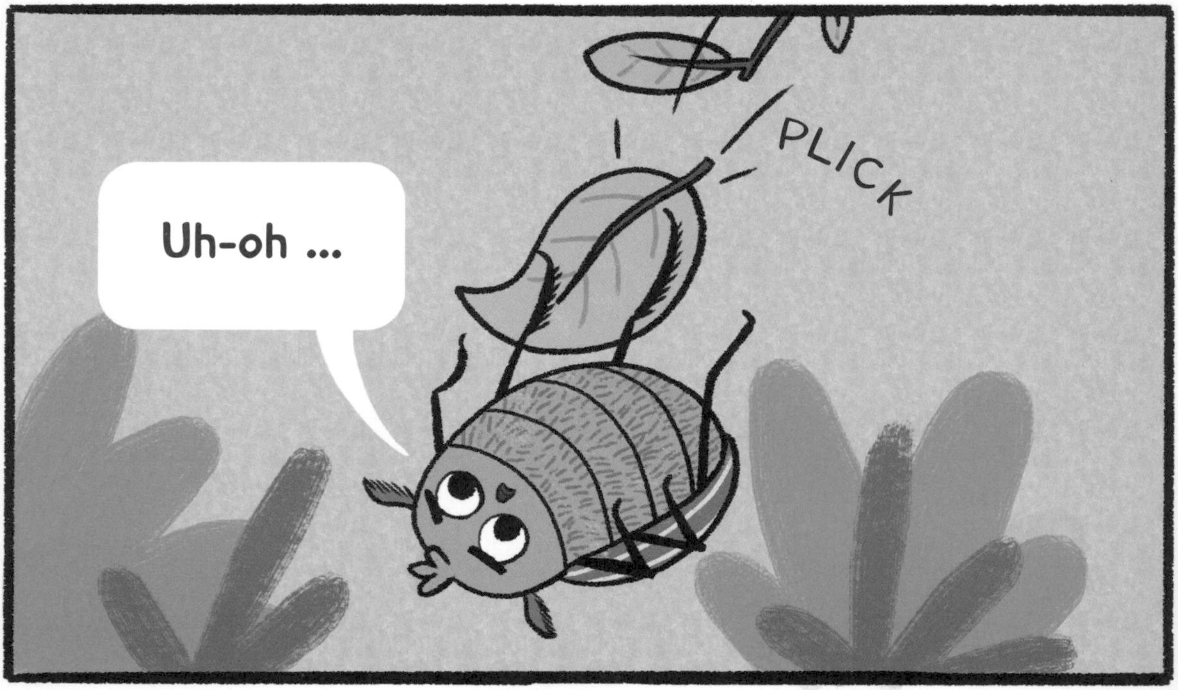
PLICK
Uh-oh ...

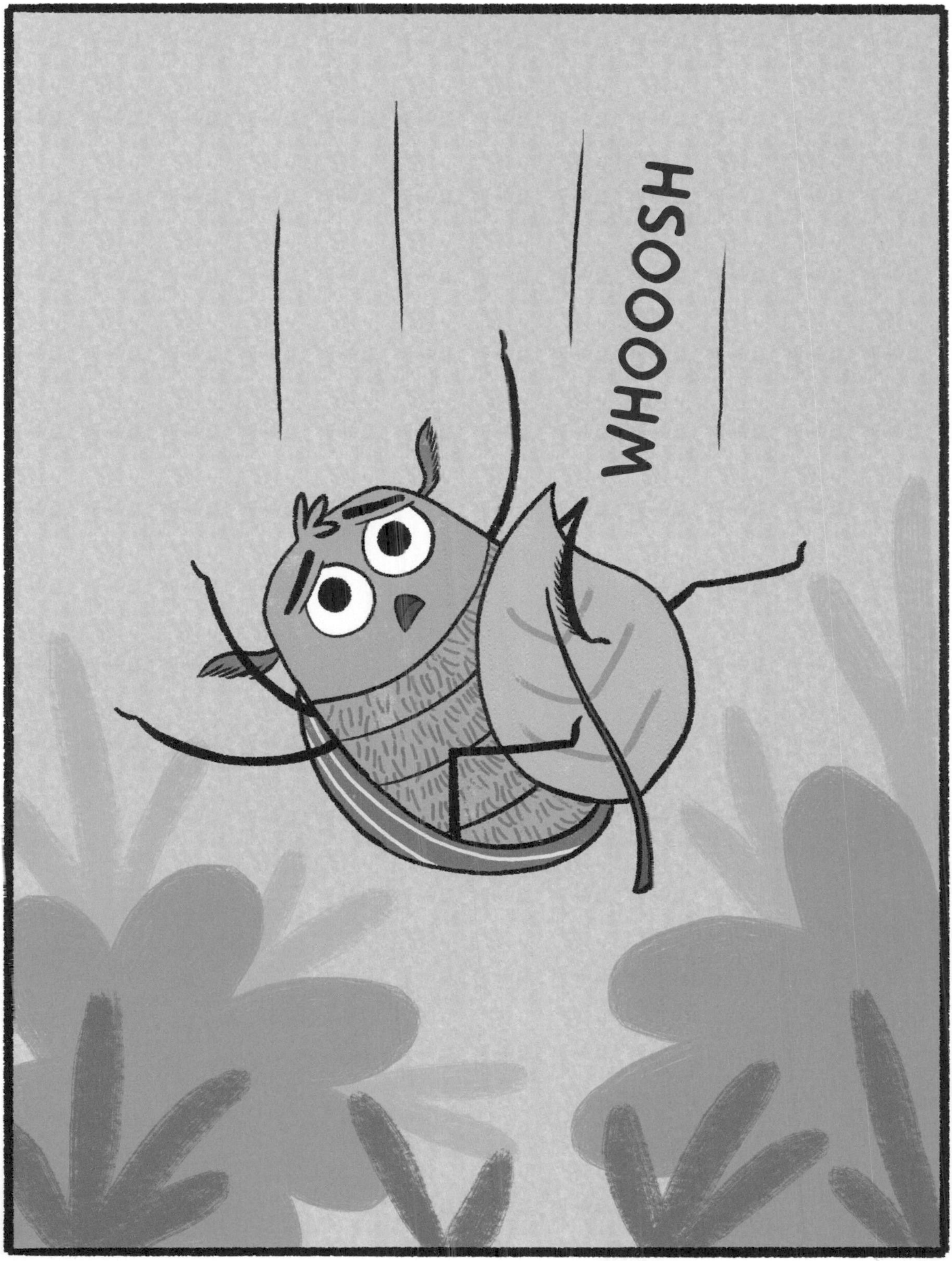
WHOOOSH

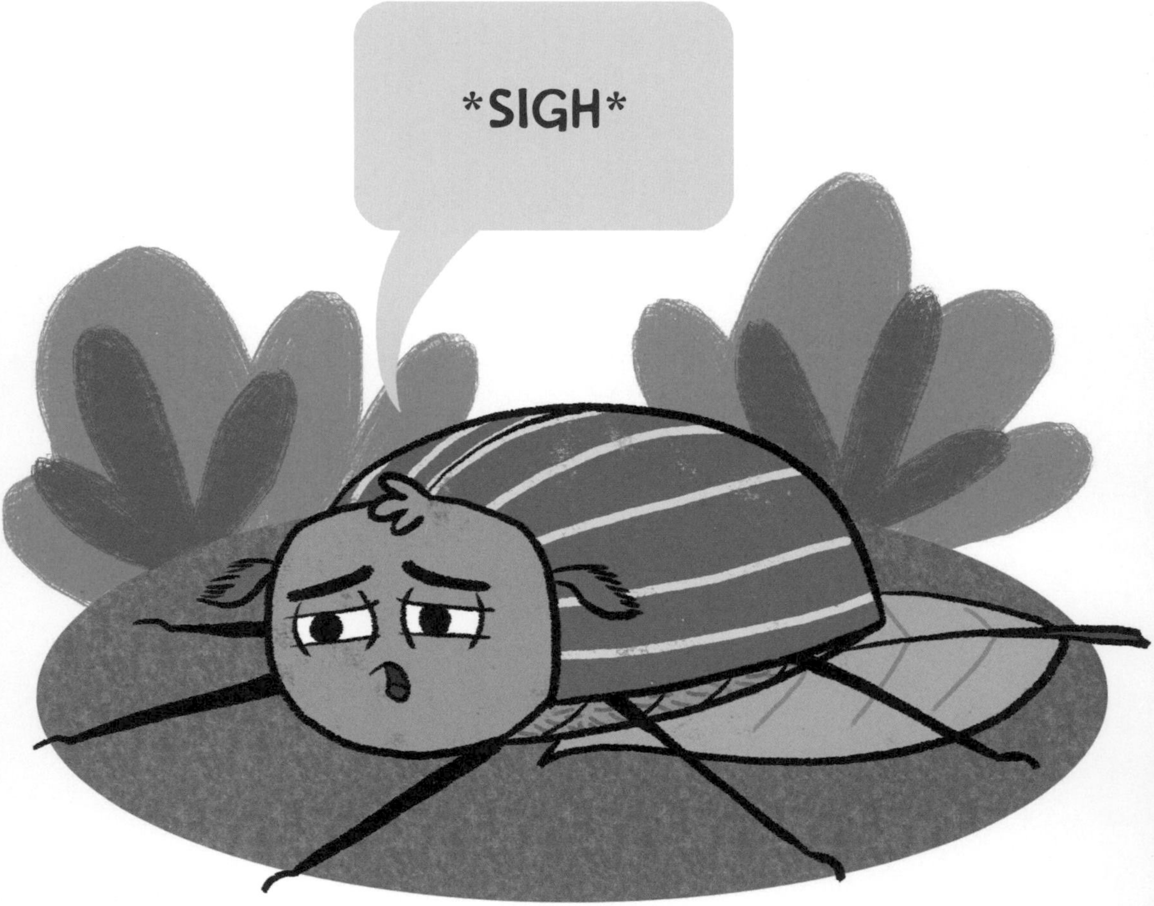
SIGH

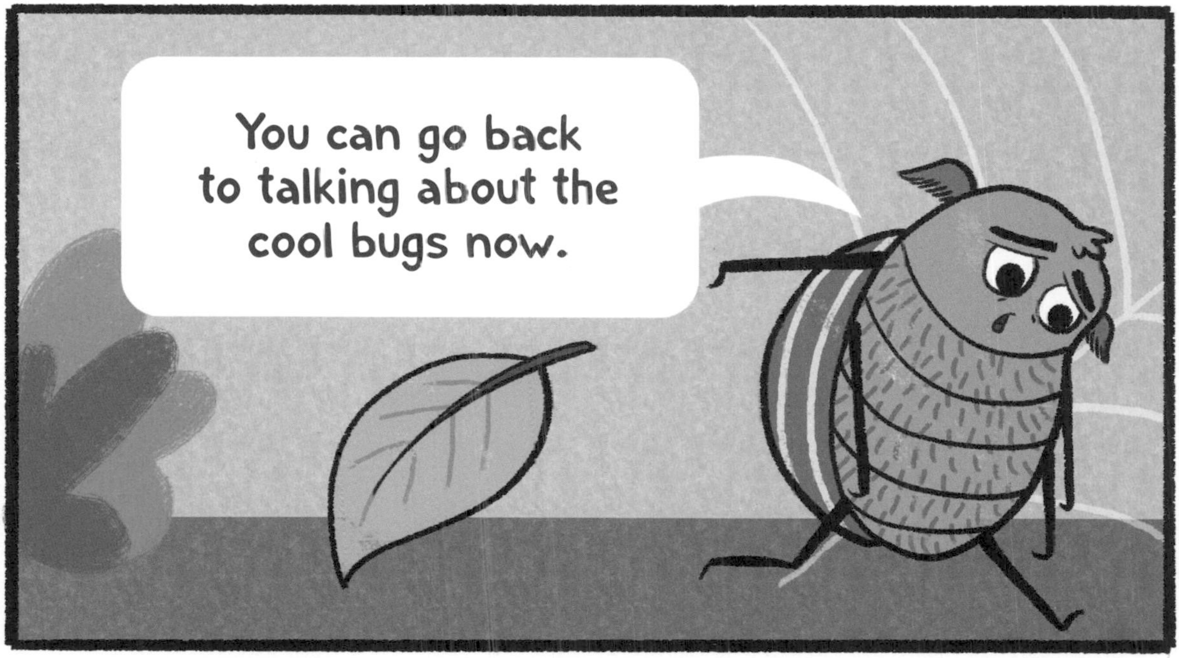
You can go back to talking about the cool bugs now.

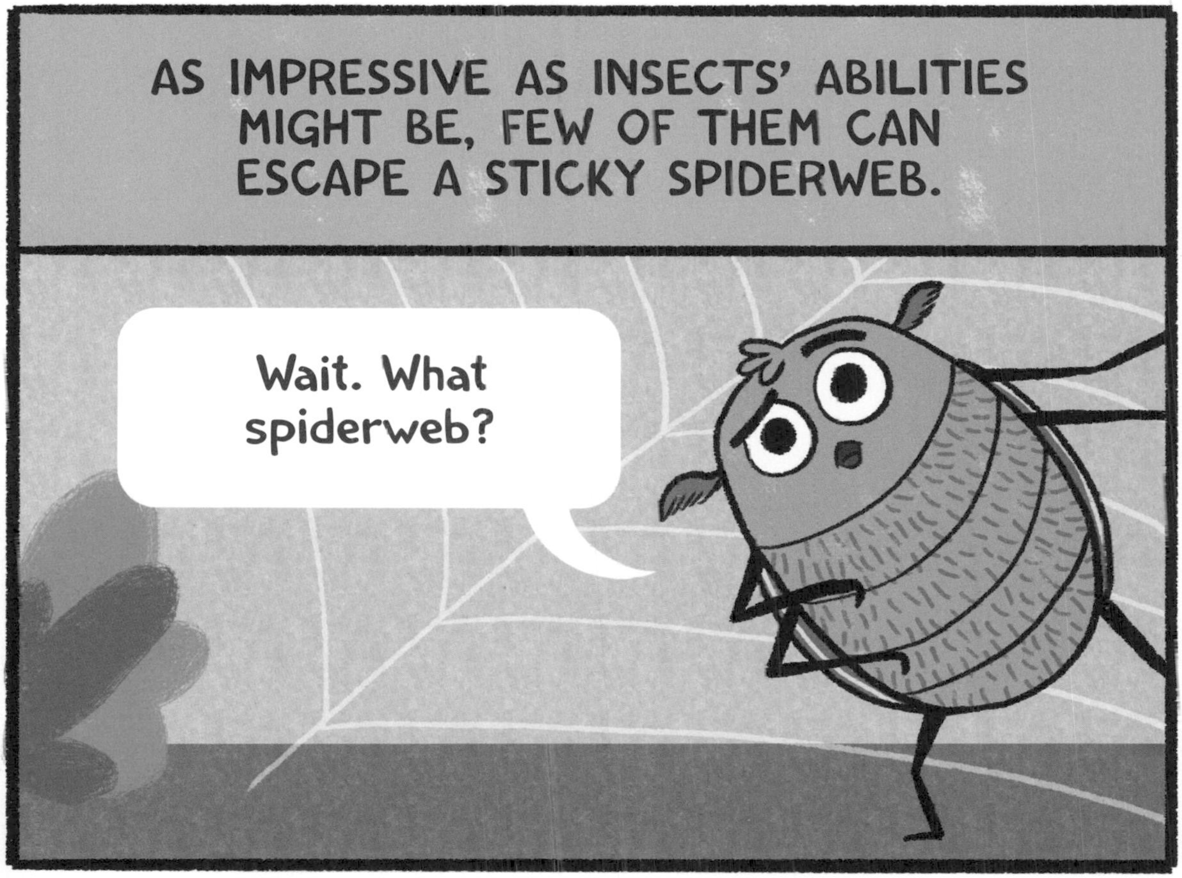
AS IMPRESSIVE AS INSECTS' ABILITIES MIGHT BE, FEW OF THEM CAN ESCAPE A STICKY SPIDERWEB.
Wait. What spiderweb?

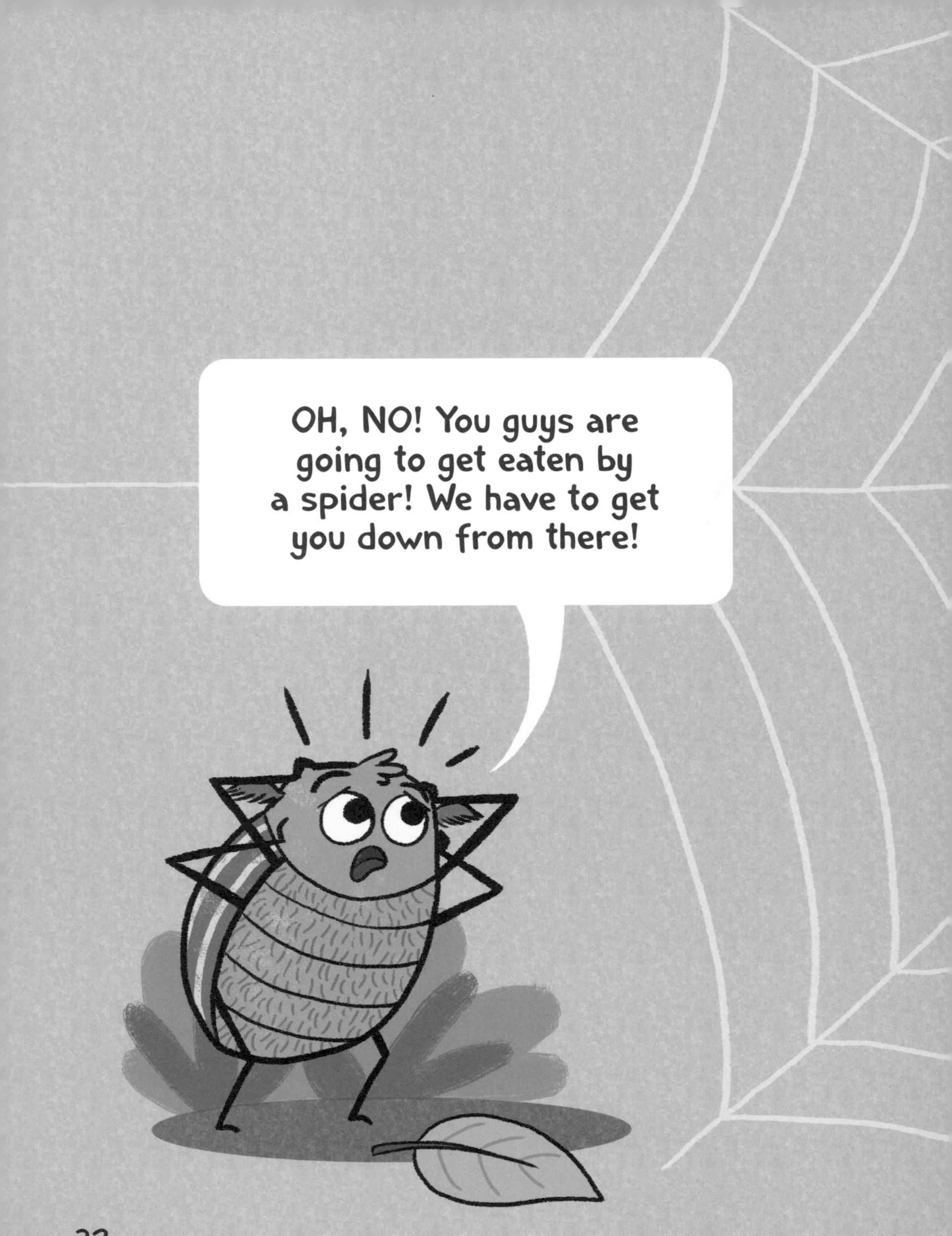
OH, NO! You guys are going to get eaten by a spider! We have to get you down from there!

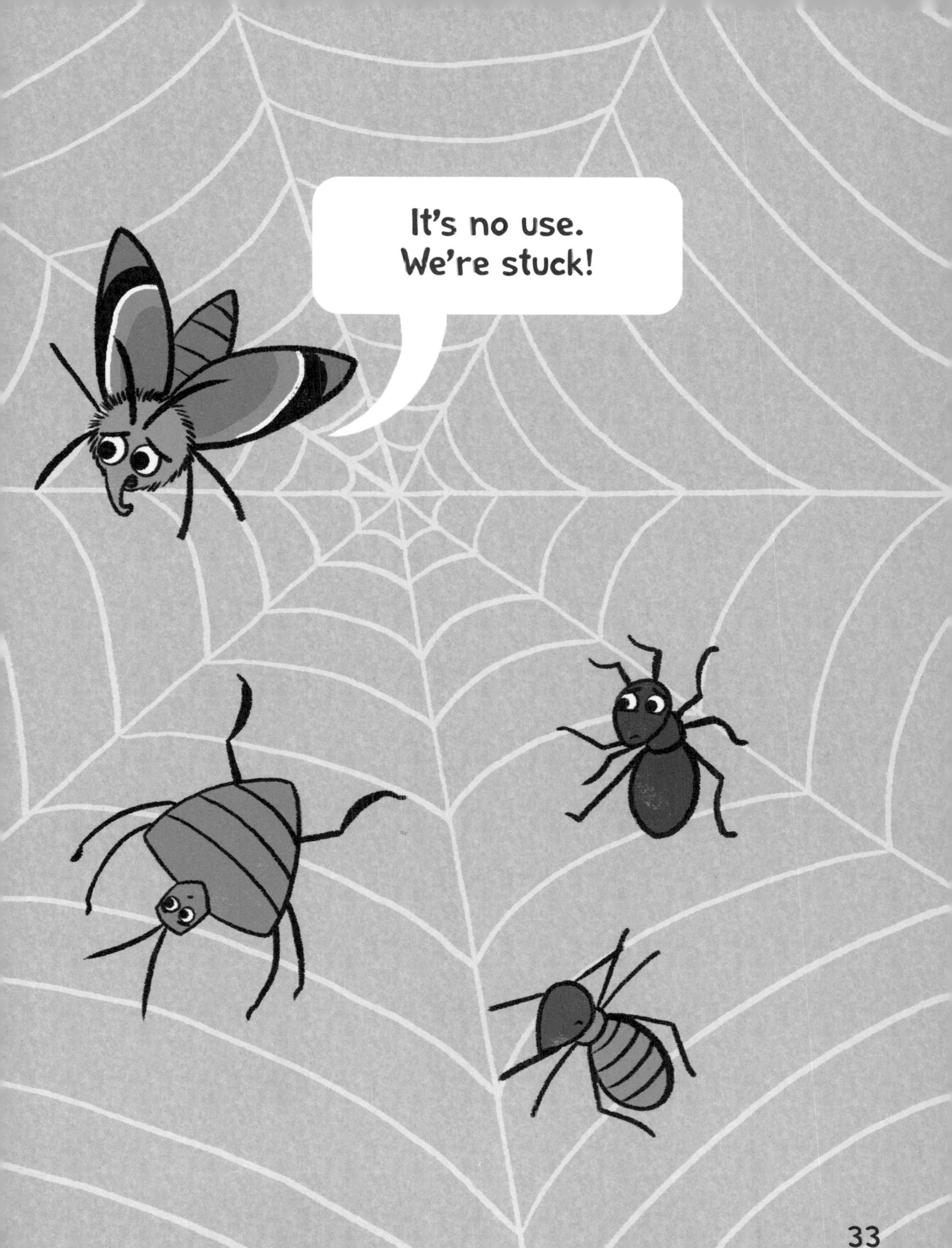
It's no use.
We're stuck!

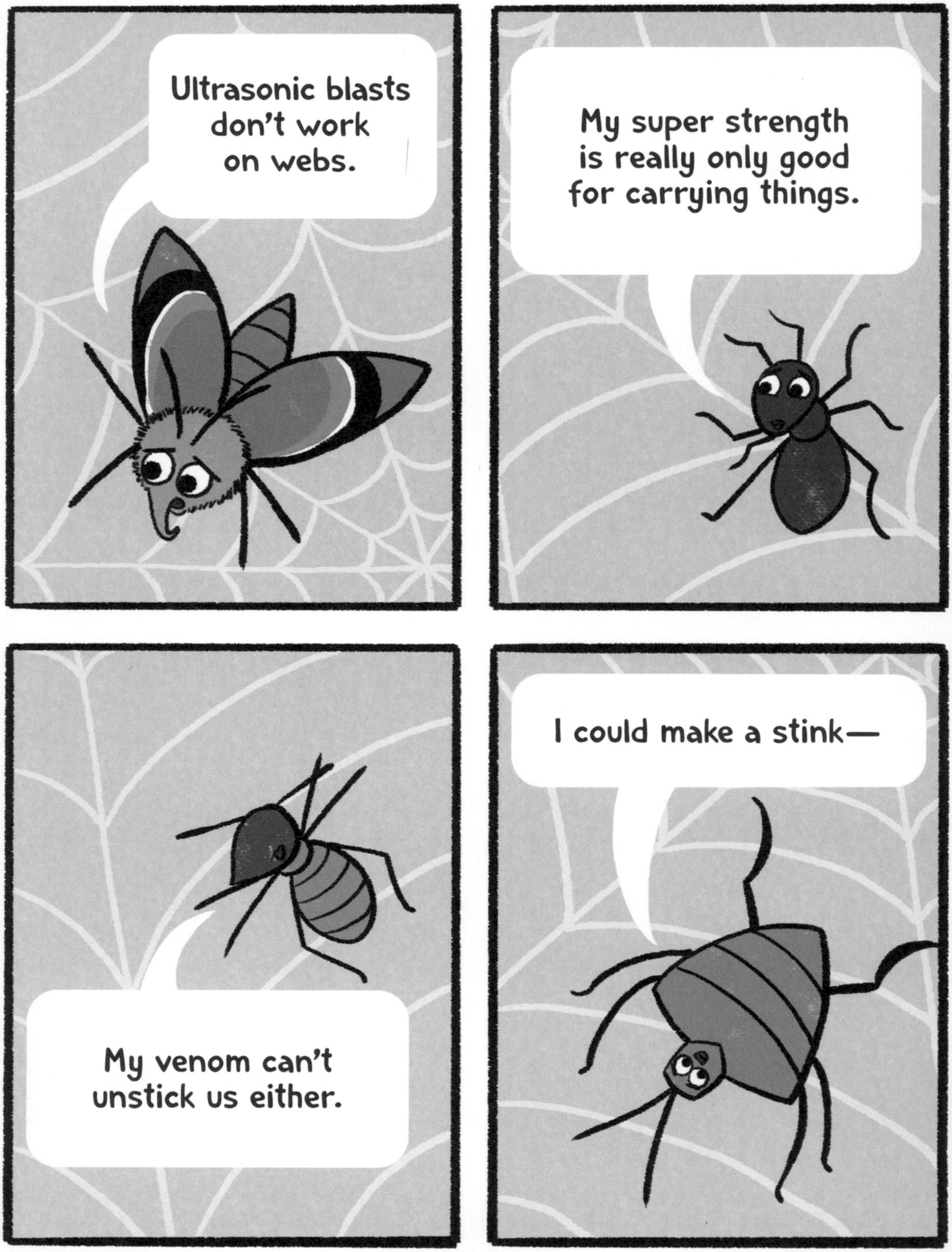
Ultrasonic blasts don't work on webs.
My super strength is really only good for carrying things.
My venom can't unstick us either.
I could make a stink—

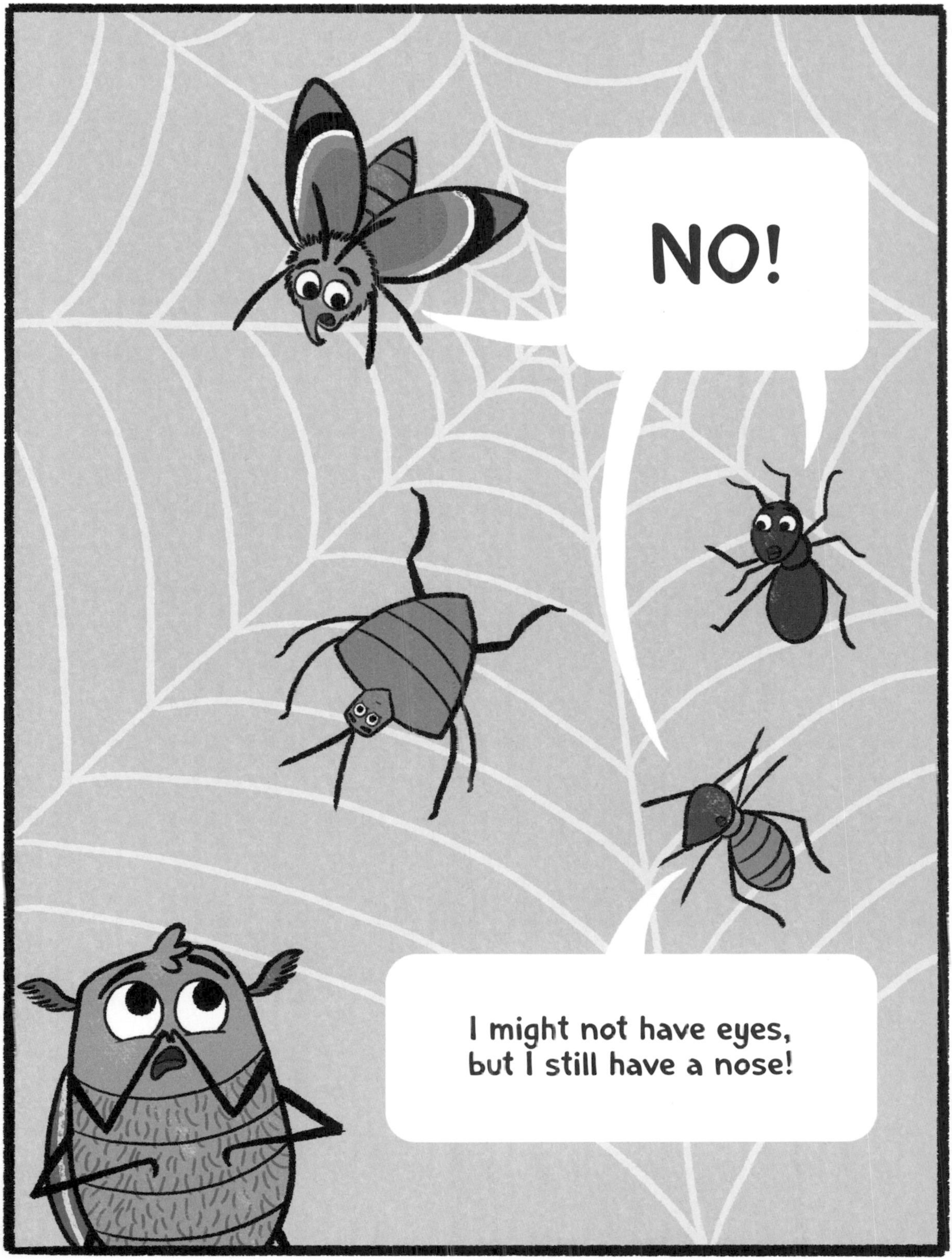
NO!
I might not have eyes,
but I still have a nose!

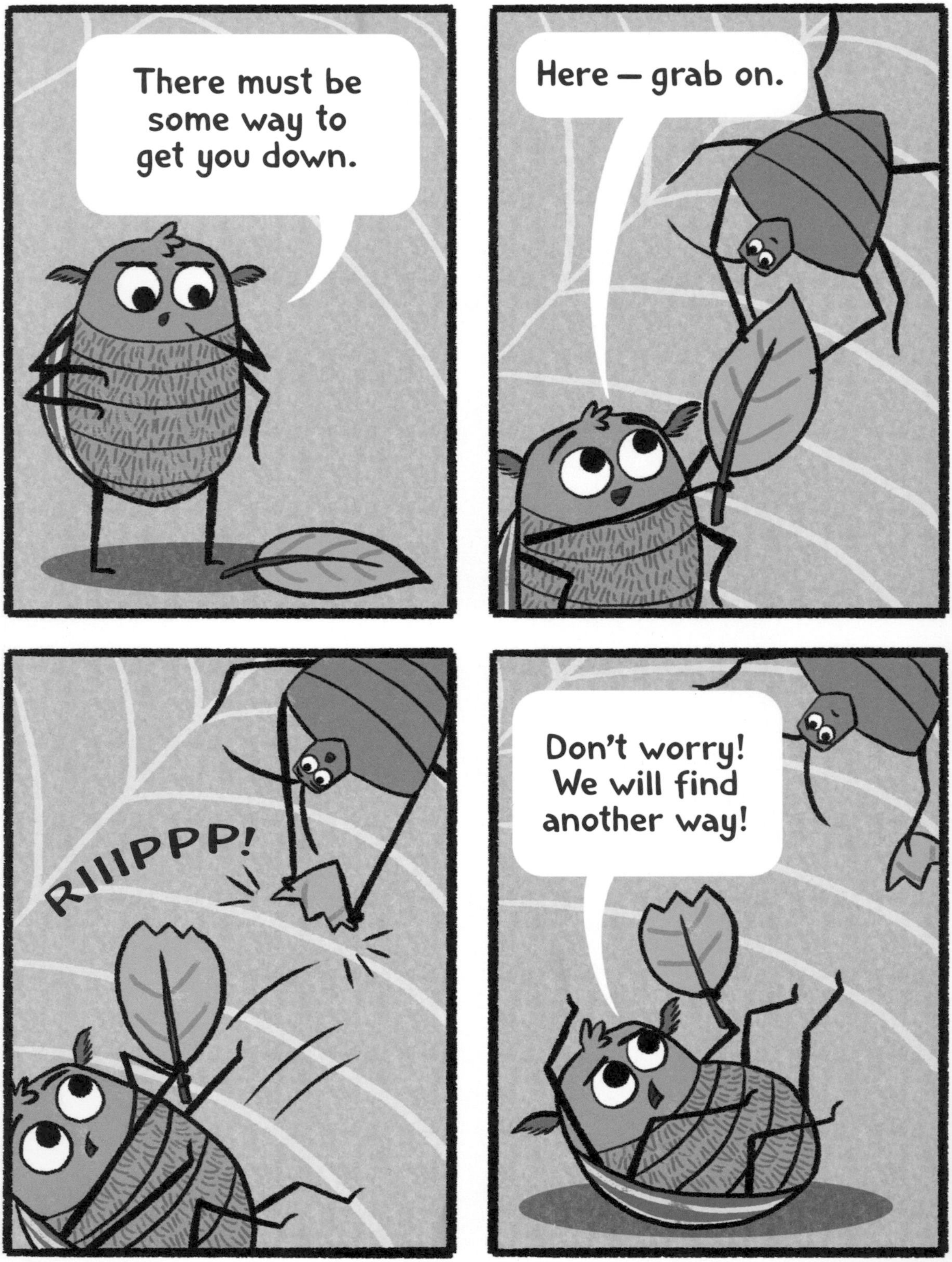
There must be some way to get you down.
Here — grab on.
RIIIPPP!
Don't worry! We will find another way!

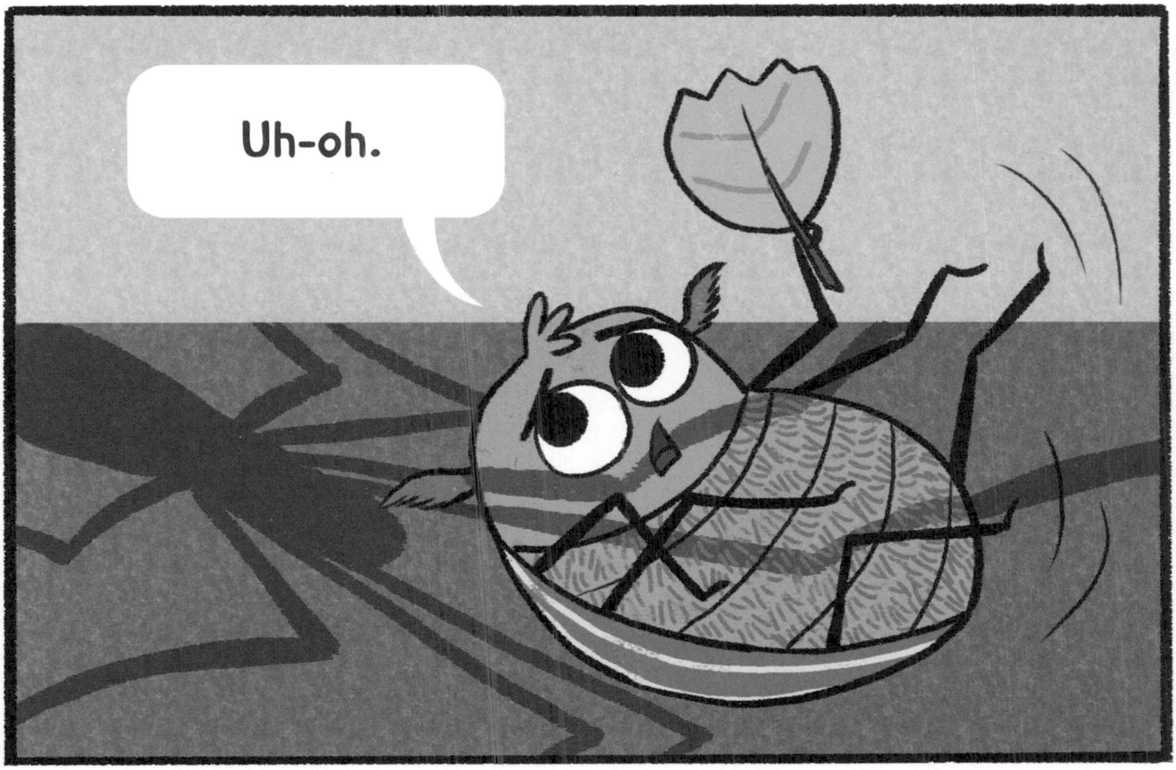
Uh-oh.

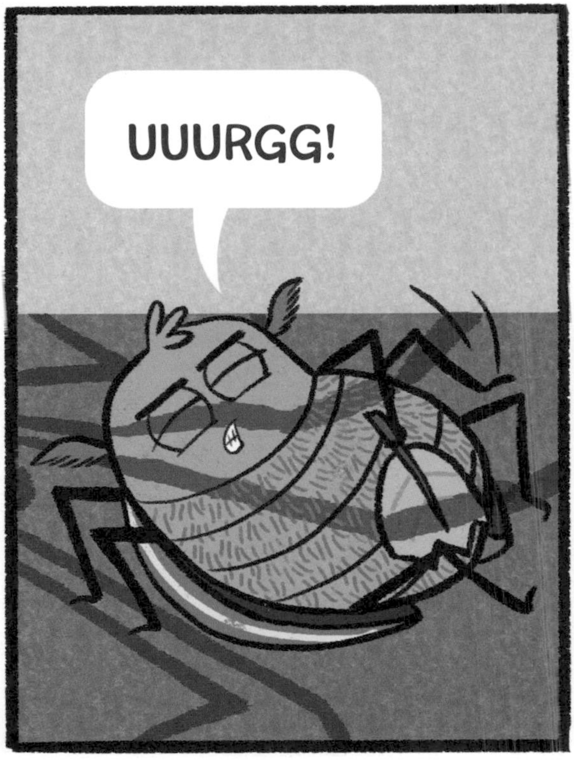
UUURGG!

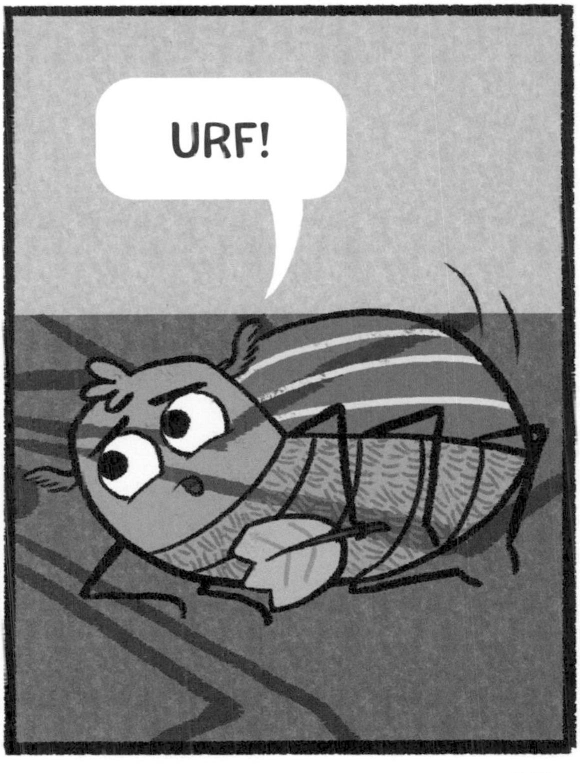
URF!

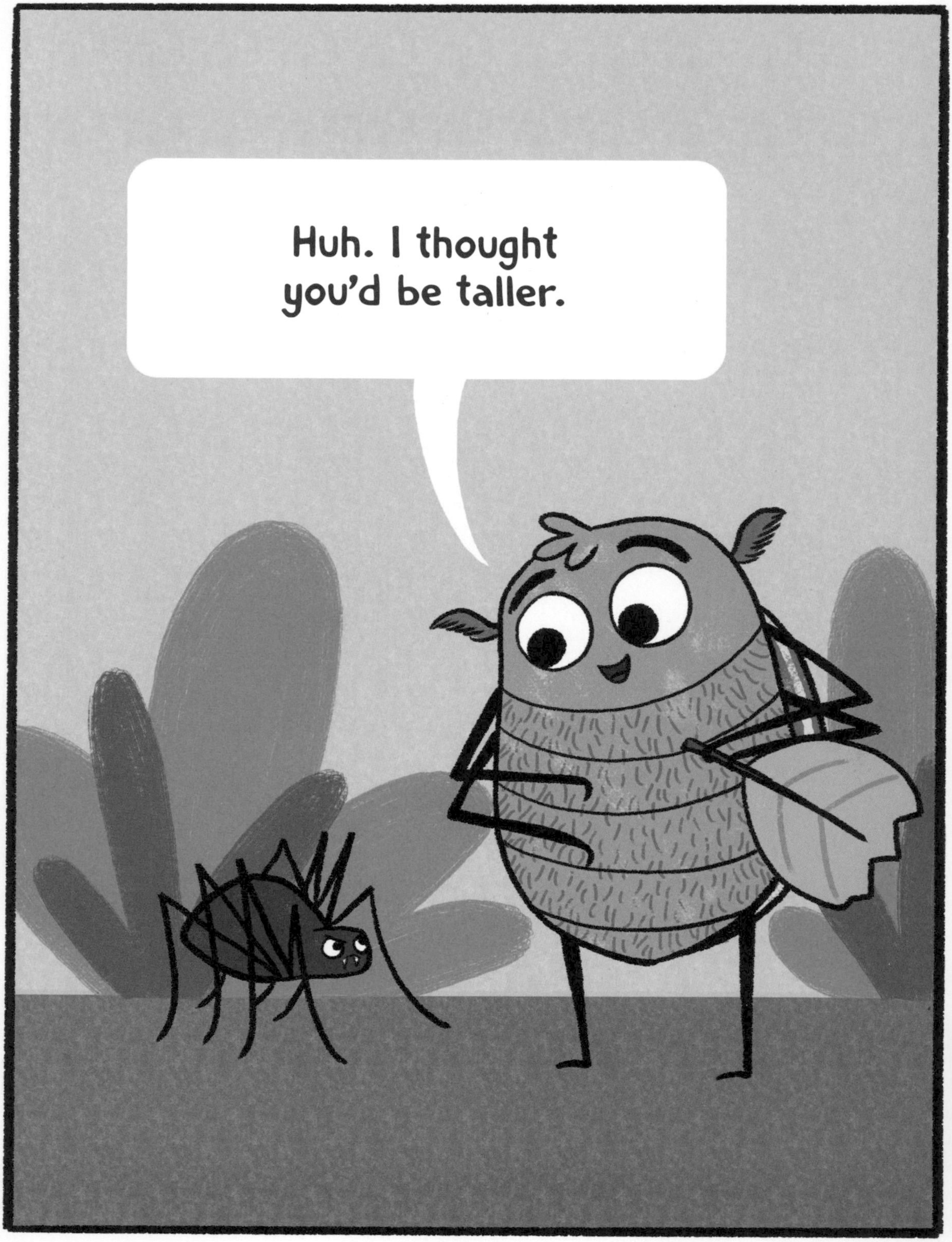
Huh. I thought you'd be taller.

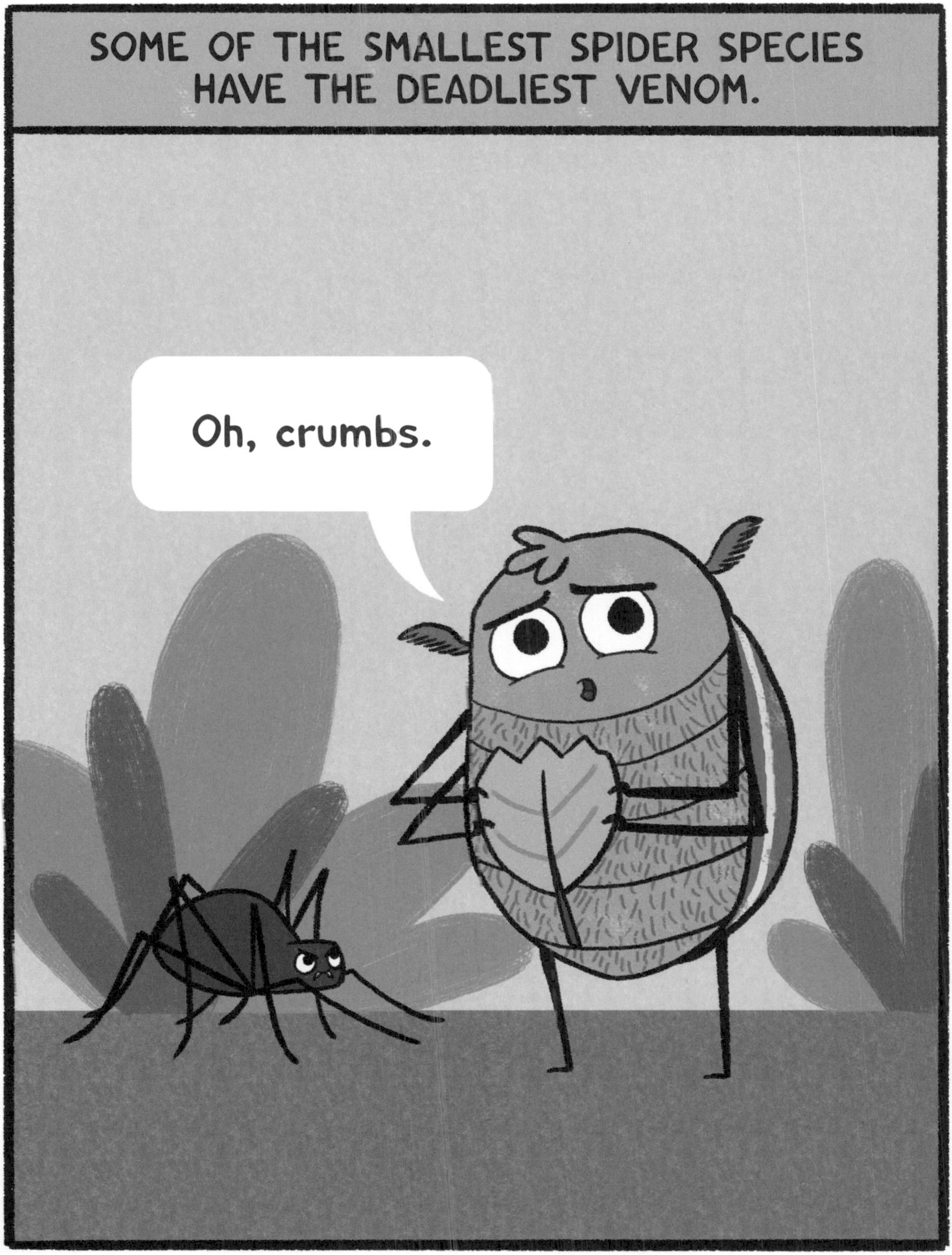
SOME OF THE SMALLEST SPIDER SPECIES HAVE THE DEADLIEST VENOM.
Oh, crumbs.

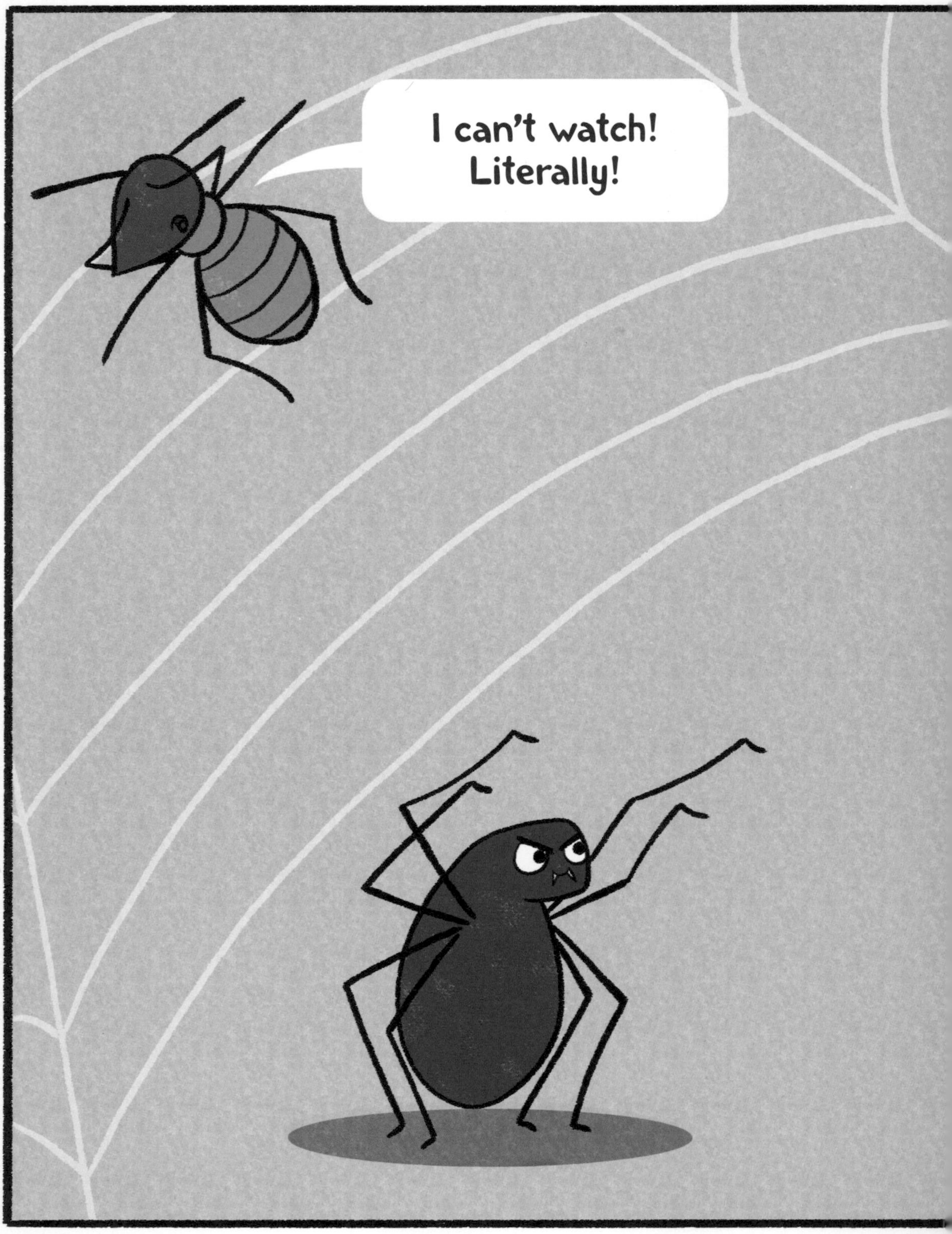
I can't watch! Literally!

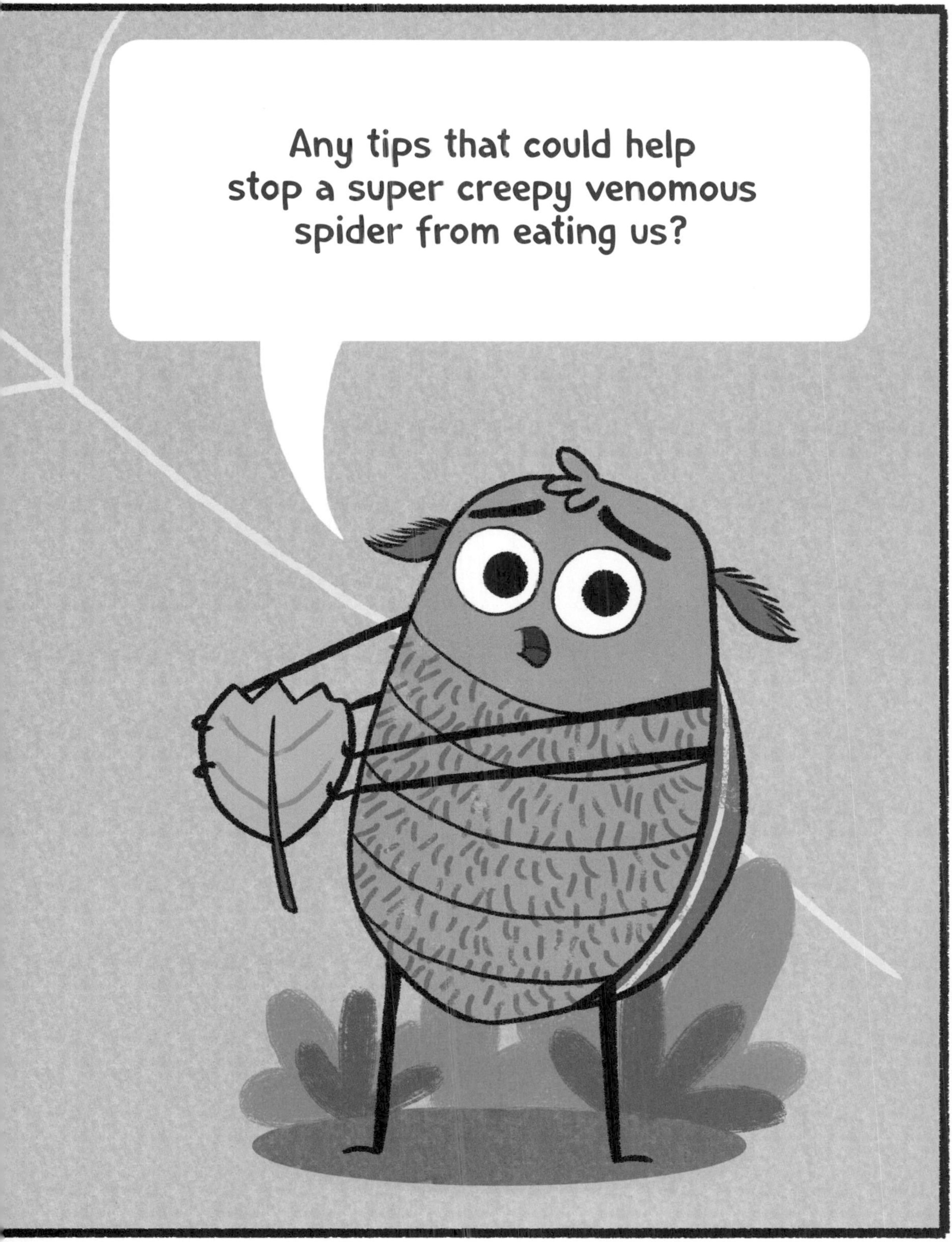
Any tips that could help stop a super creepy venomous spider from eating us?

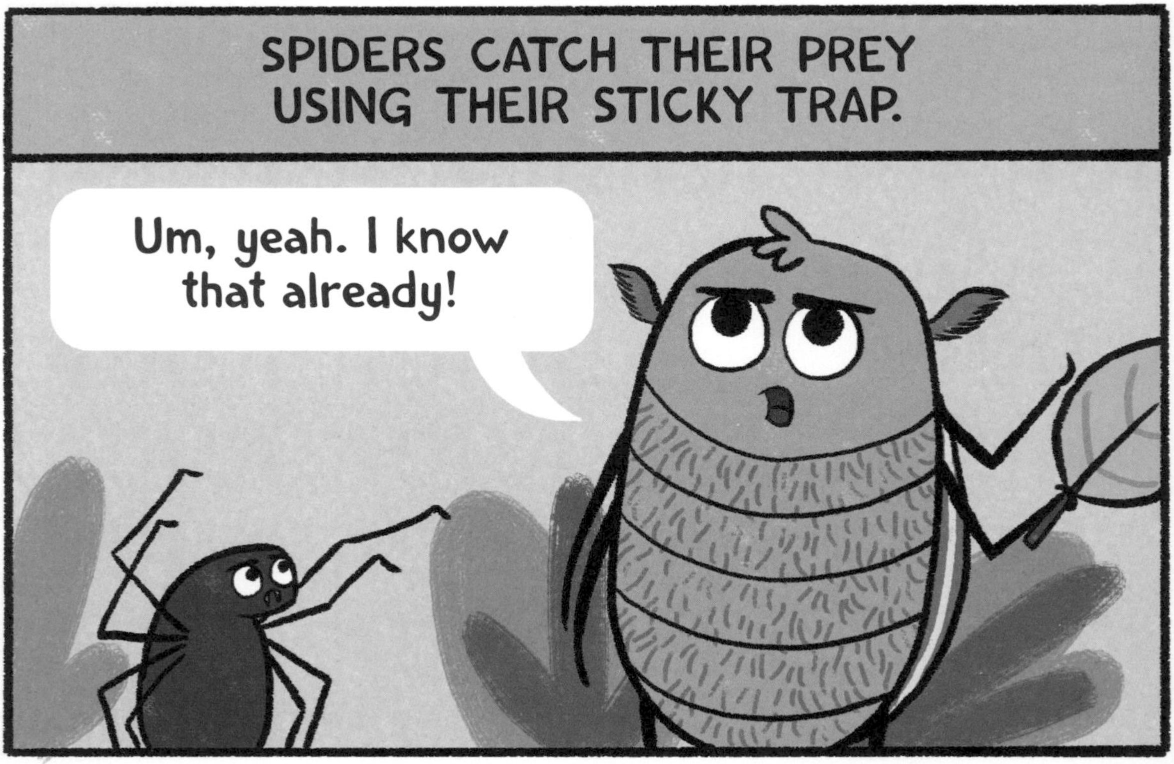
SPIDERS CATCH THEIR PREY
USING THEIR STICKY TRAP.
Um, yeah. I know that already!

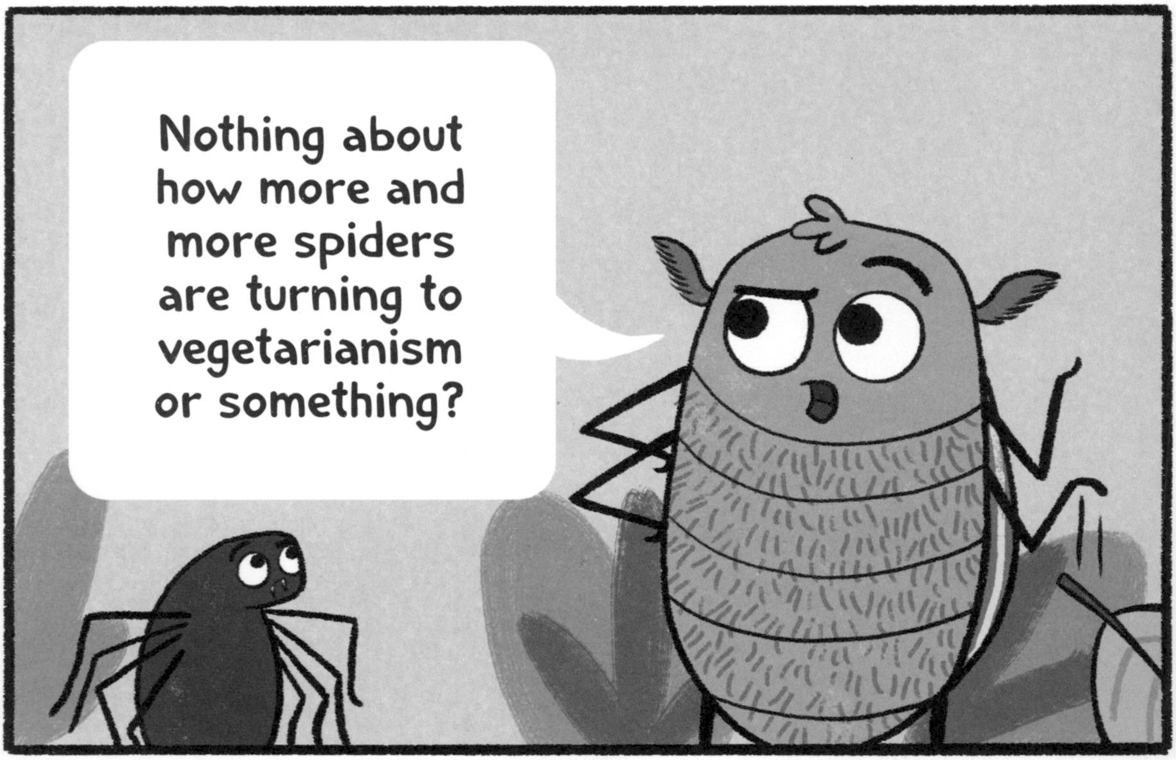
Nothing about how more and more spiders are turning to vegetarianism or something?

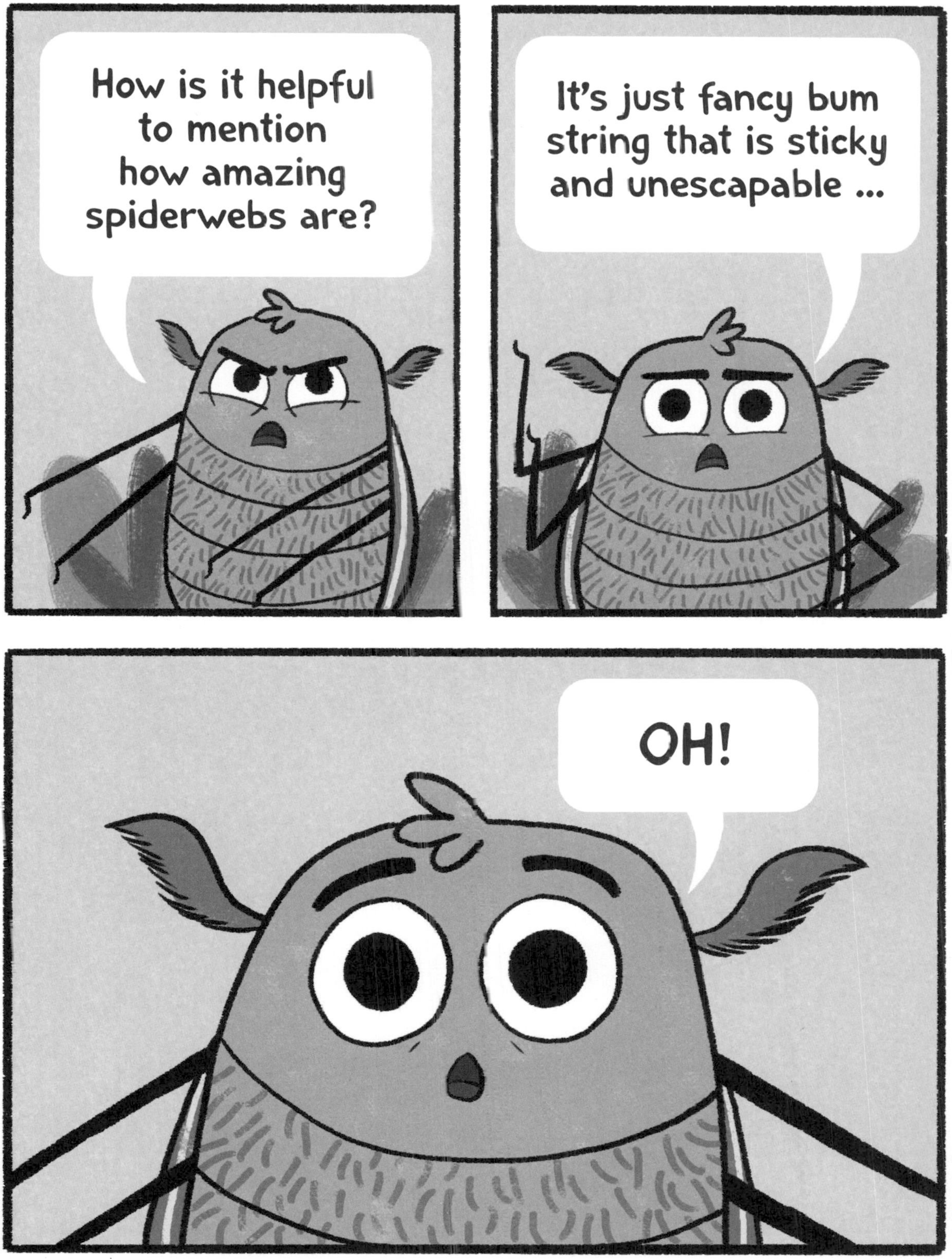
How is it helpful to mention how amazing spiderwebs are?
It's just fancy bum string that is sticky and unescapable ...
OH!

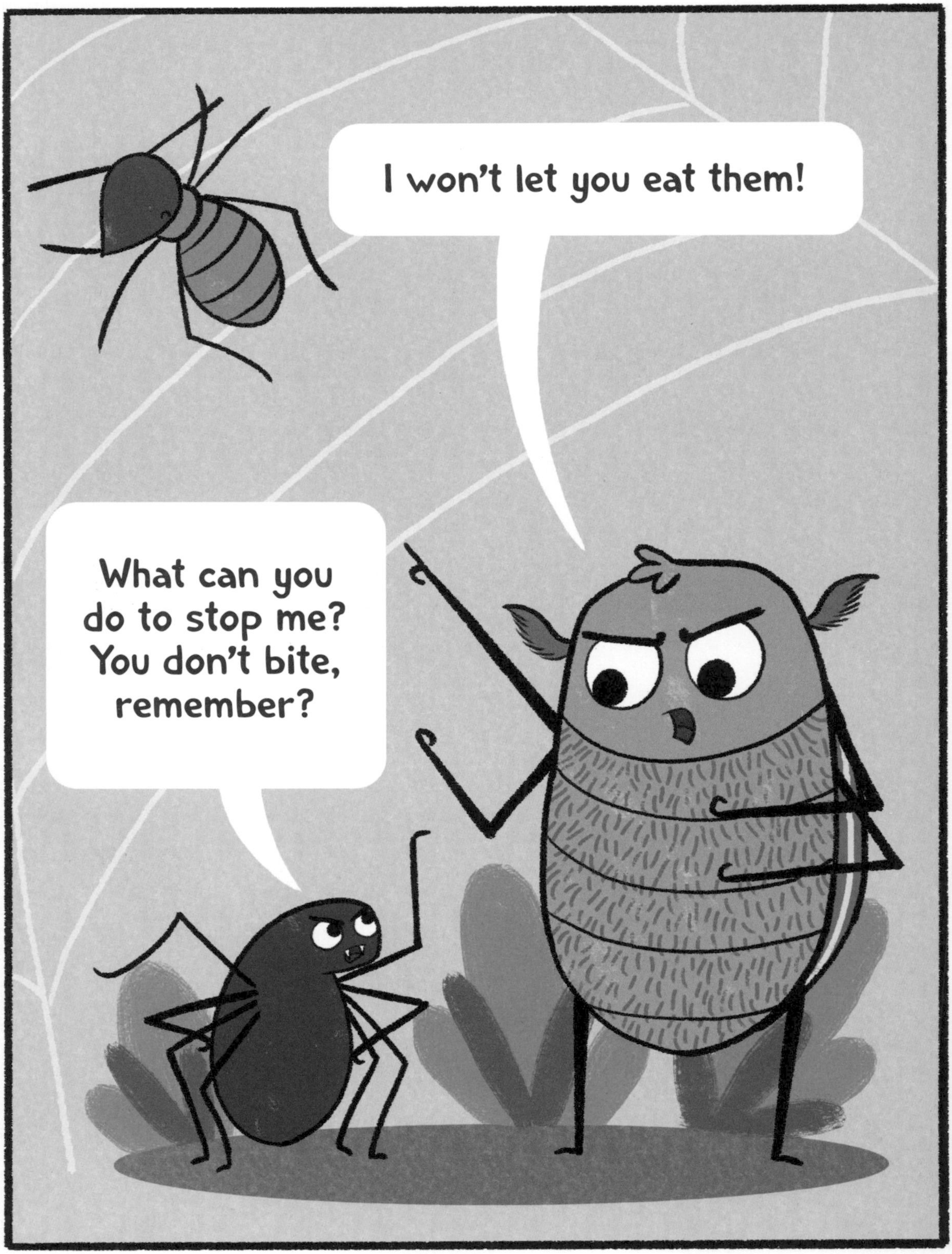
I won't let you eat them!
What can you do to stop me? You don't bite, remember?

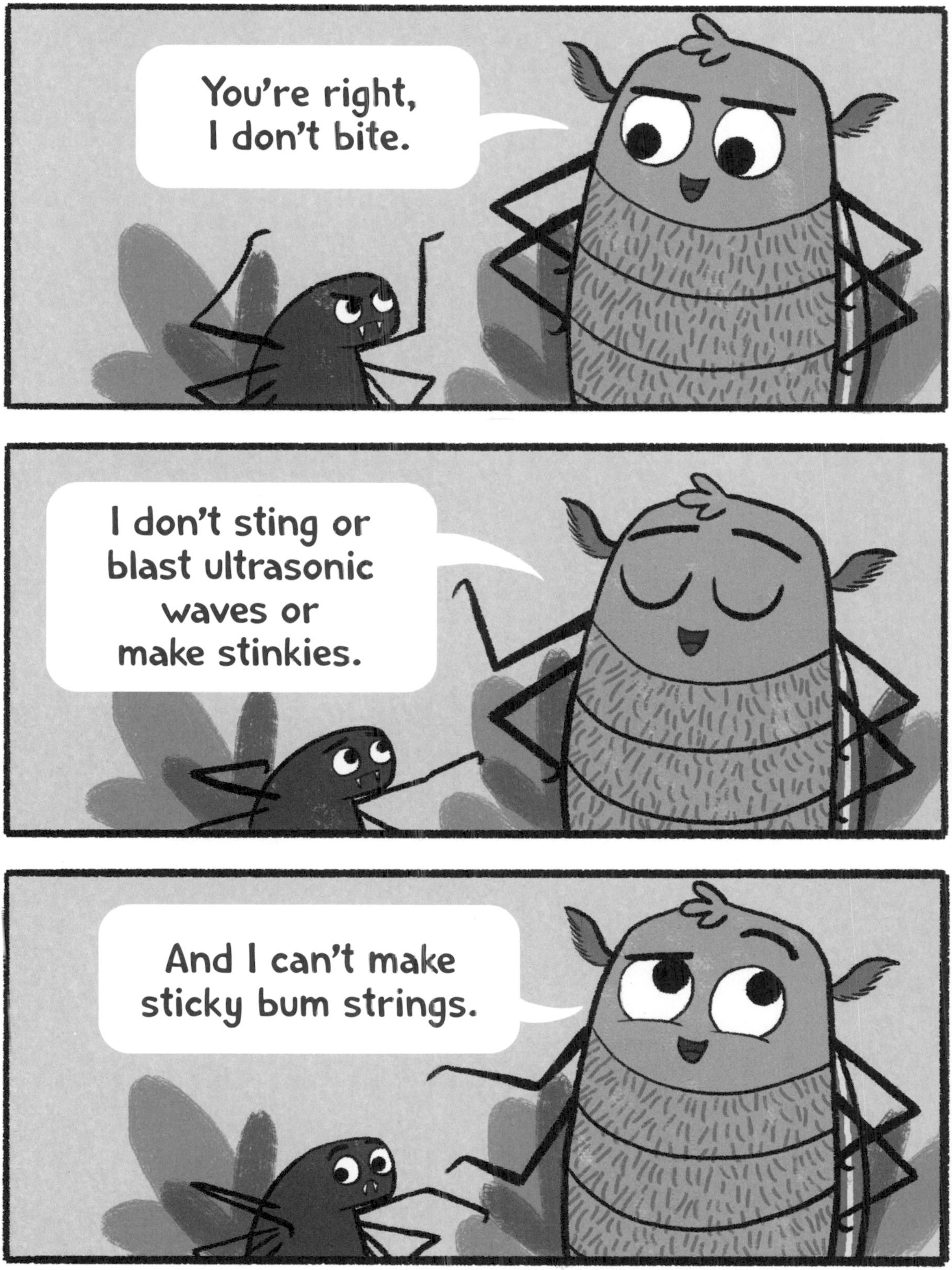

You're right, I don't bite.
I don't sting or blast ultrasonic waves or make stinkies.
And I can't make sticky bum strings.

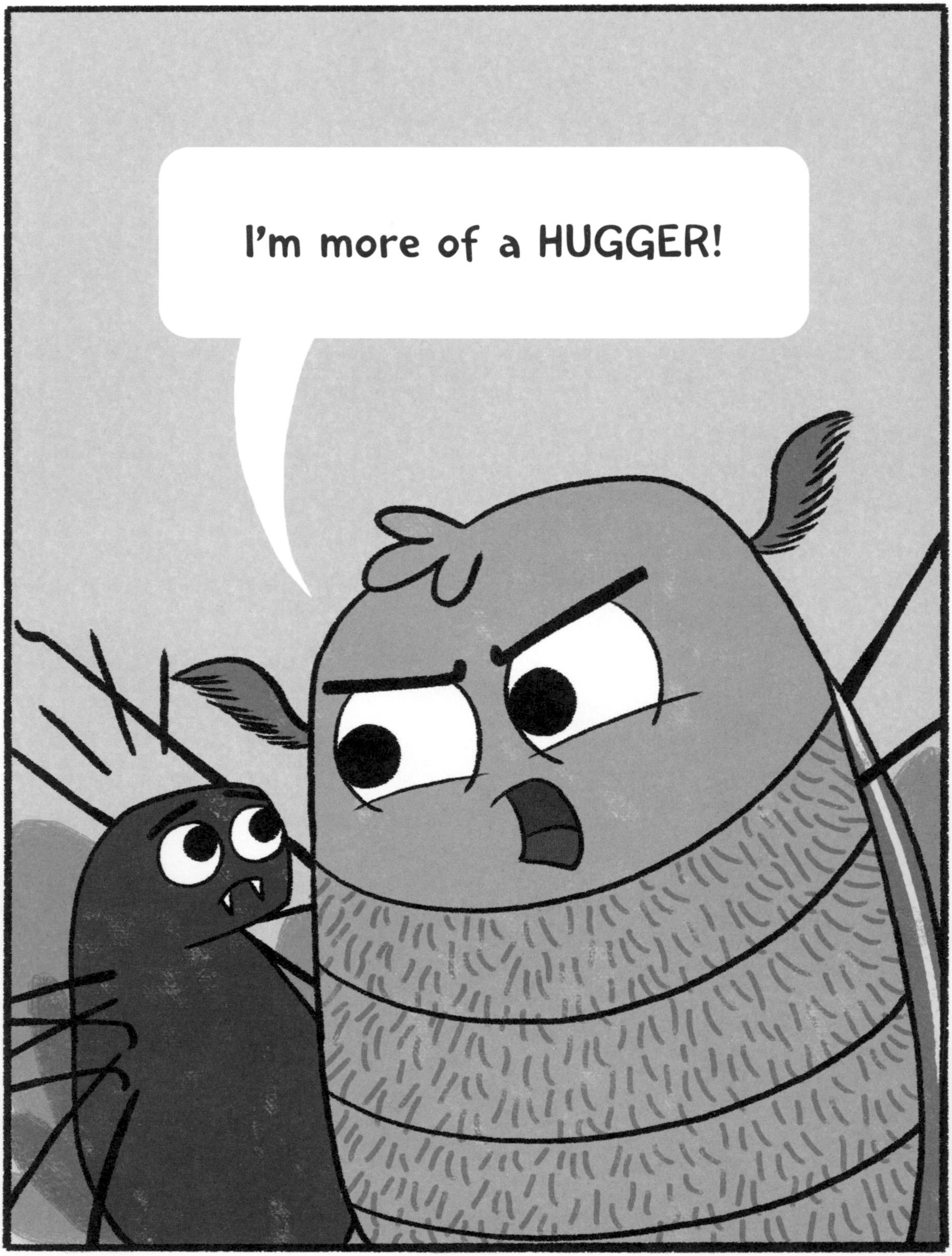
I'm more of a HUGGER!

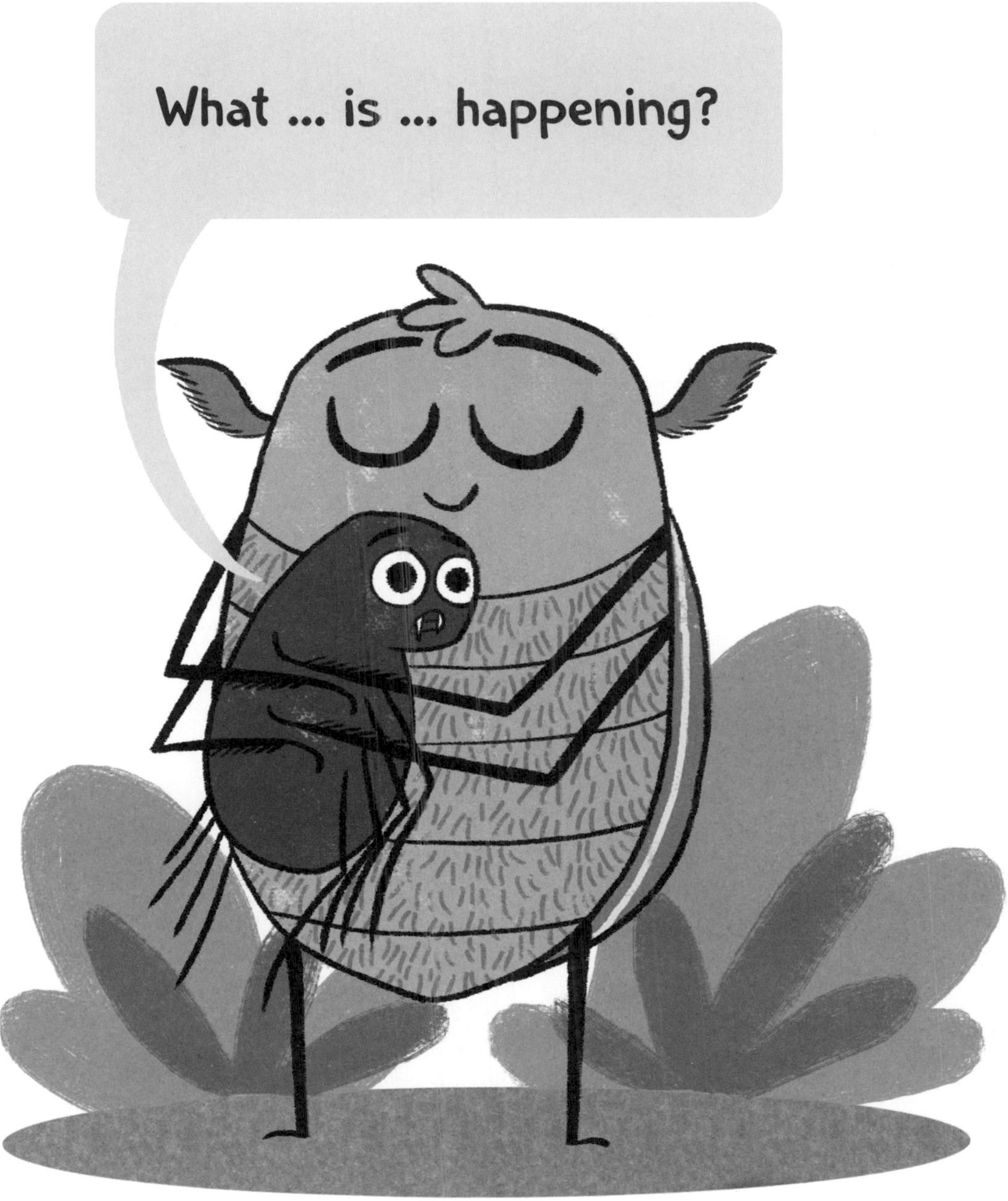
What ... is ... happening?

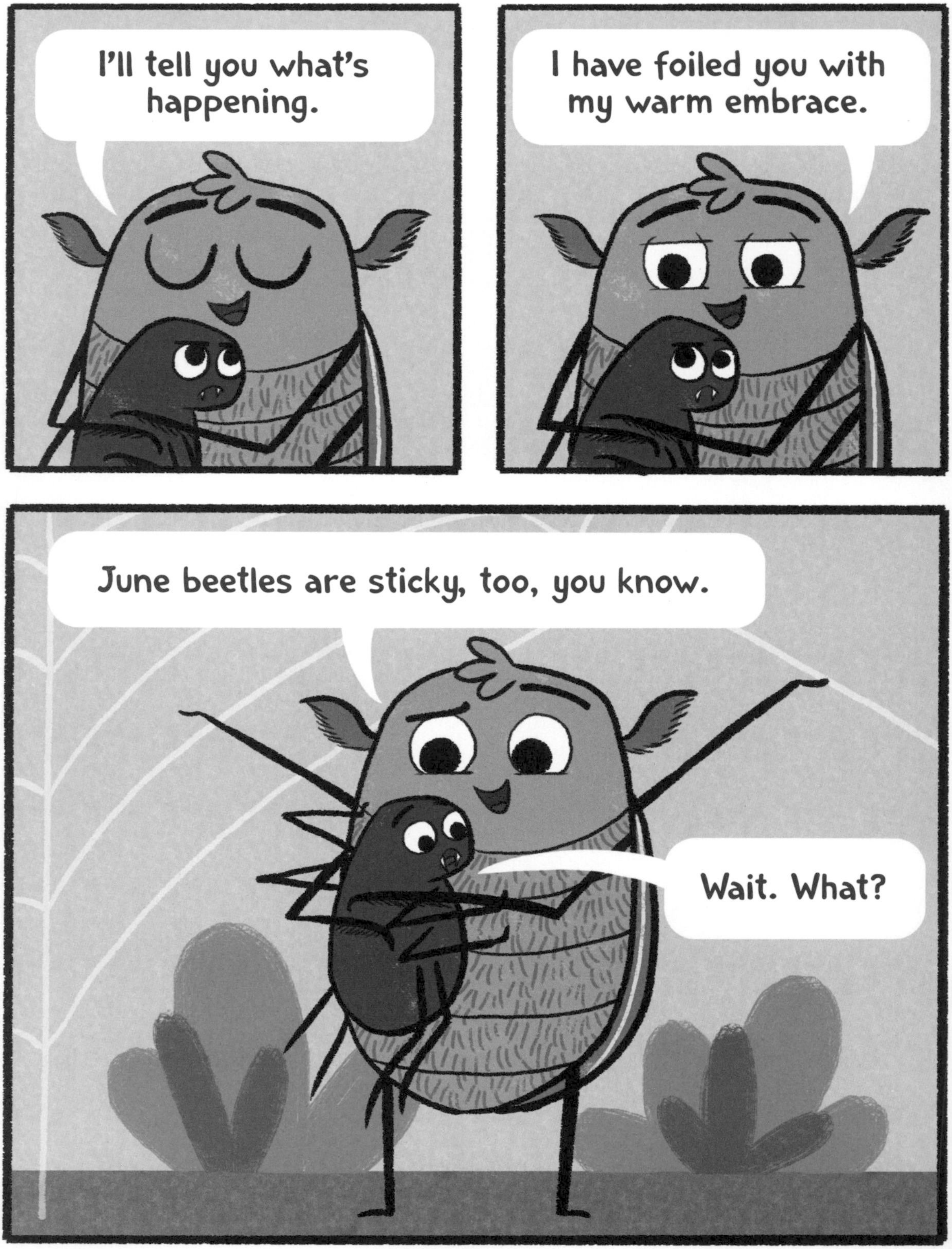
I'll tell you what's happening.
I have foiled you with my warm embrace.
June beetles are sticky, too, you know.
Wait. What?

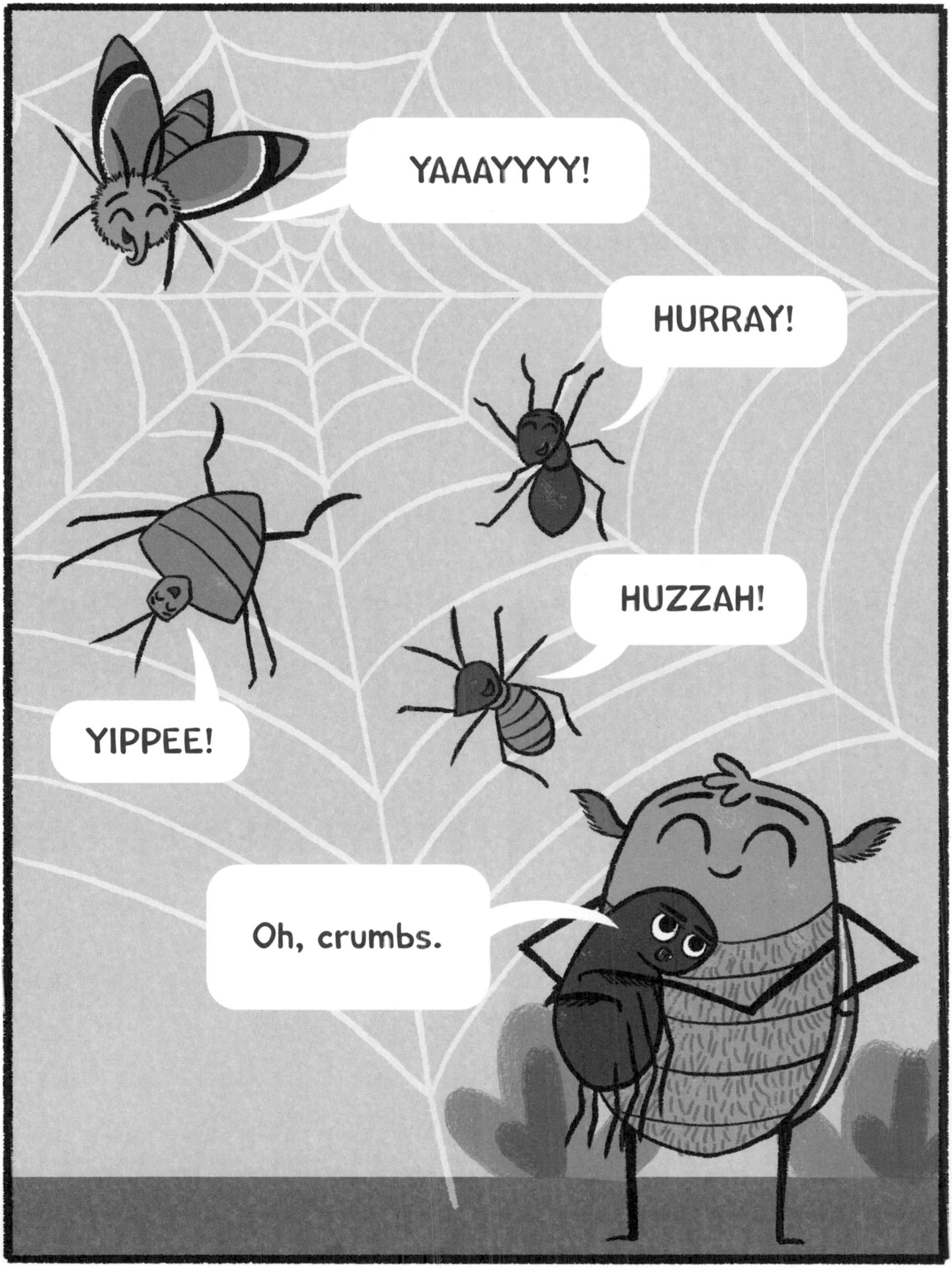
YAAAYYYY!
HURRAY!
HUZZAH!
YIPPEE!
Oh, crumbs.

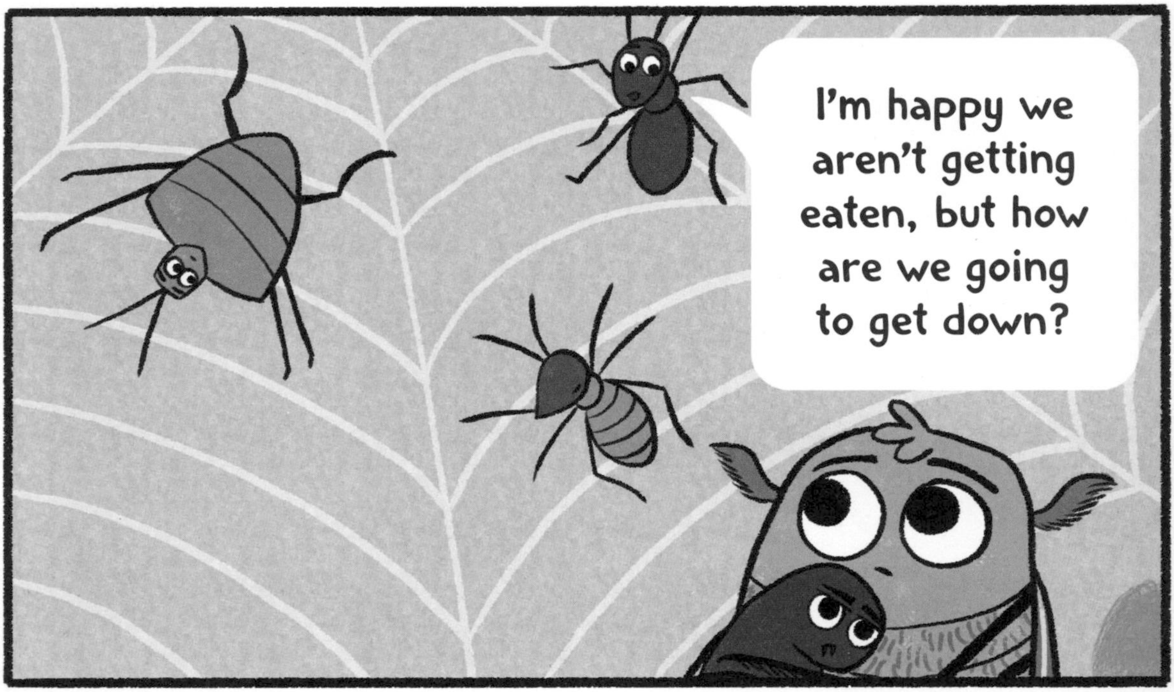
I'm happy we aren't getting eaten, but how are we going to get down?

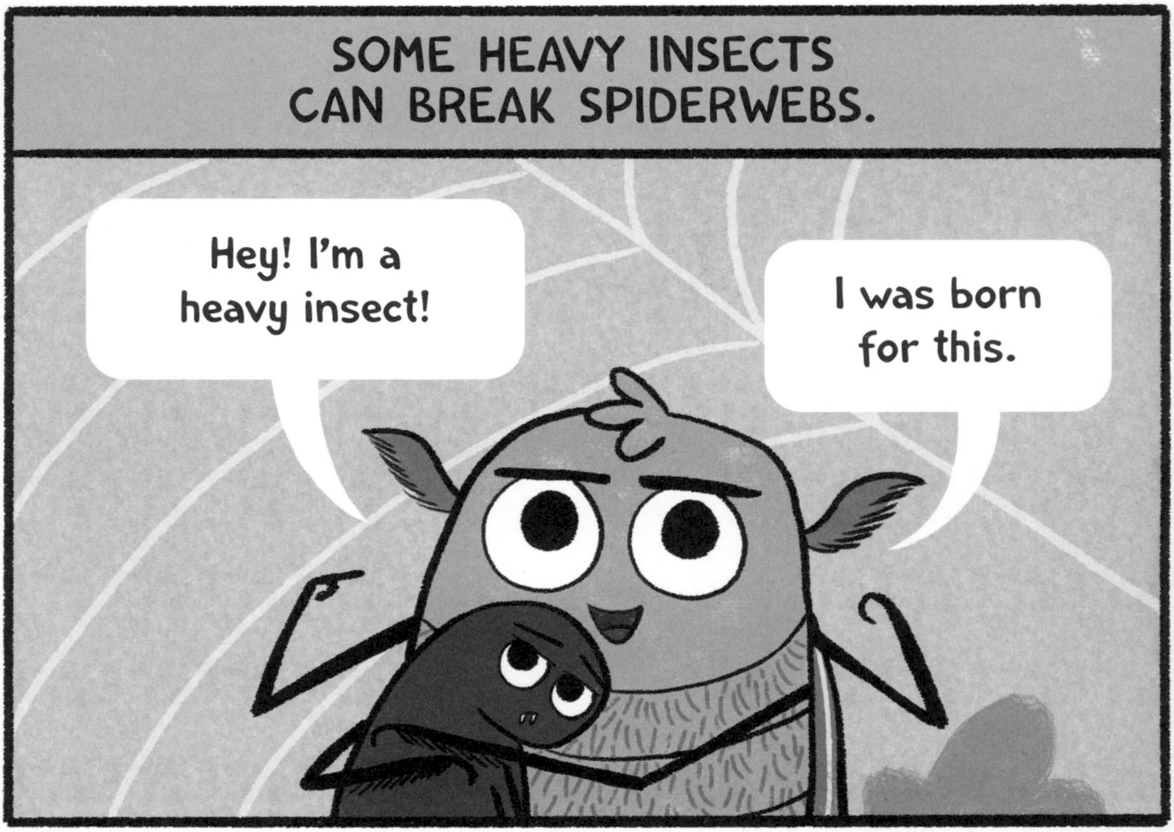
SOME HEAVY INSECTS CAN BREAK SPIDERWEBS.
Hey! I'm a heavy insect!
I was born for this.

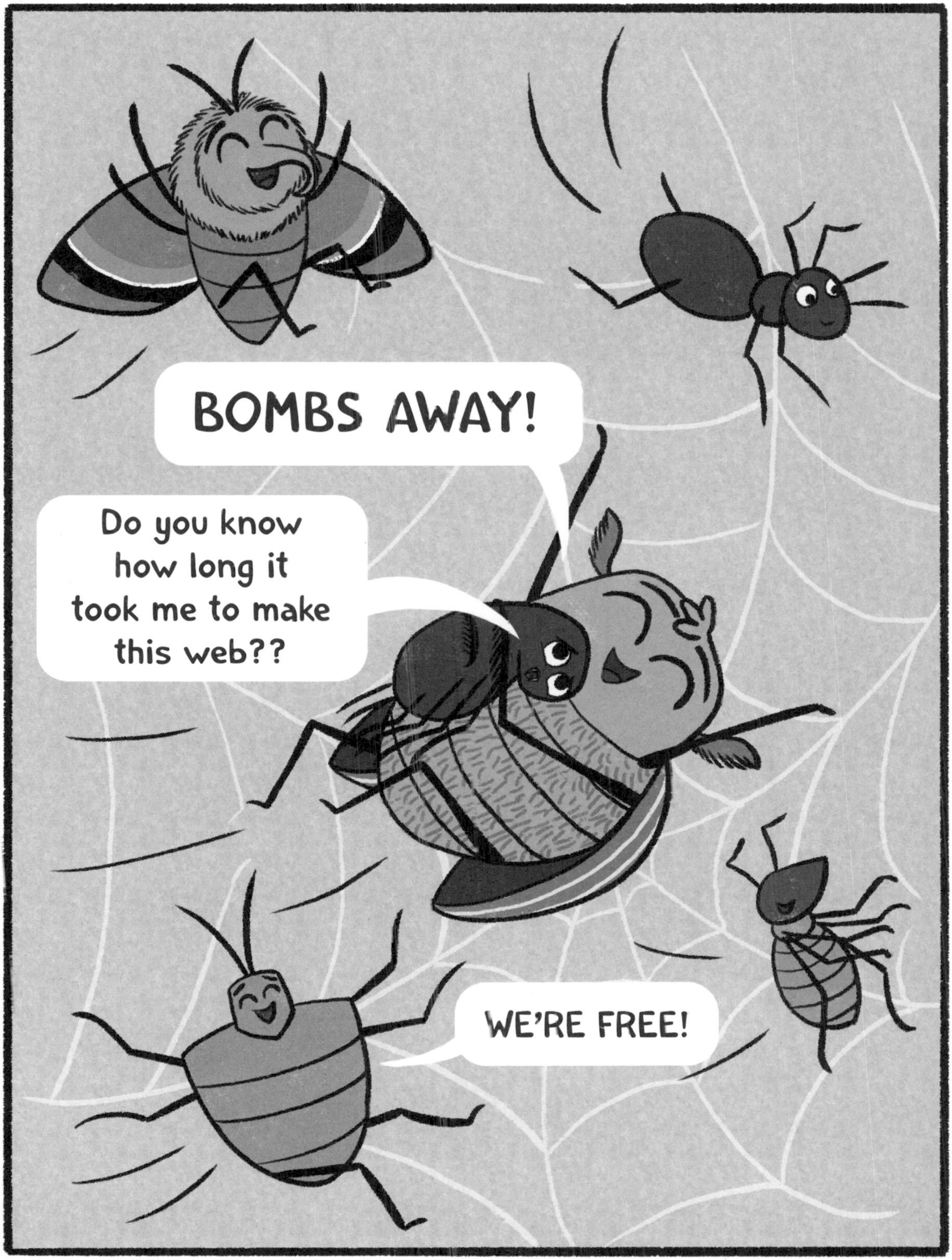
BOMBS AWAY!
Do you know how long it took me to make this web??
WE'RE FREE!

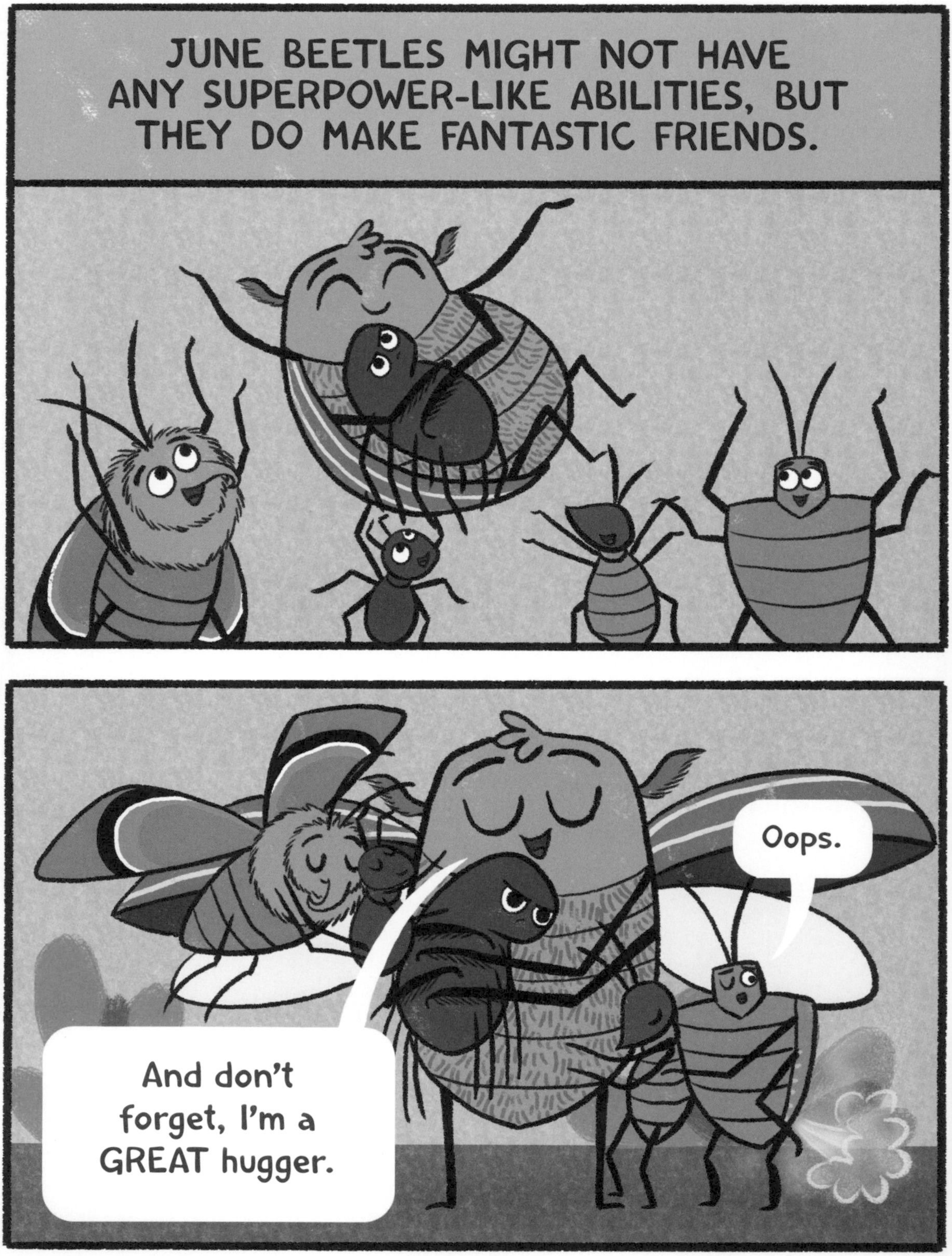
JUNE BEETLES MIGHT NOT HAVE ANY SUPERPOWER-LIKE ABILITIES, BUT THEY DO MAKE FANTASTIC FRIENDS.
Oops.
And don't forget, I'm a GREAT hugger.

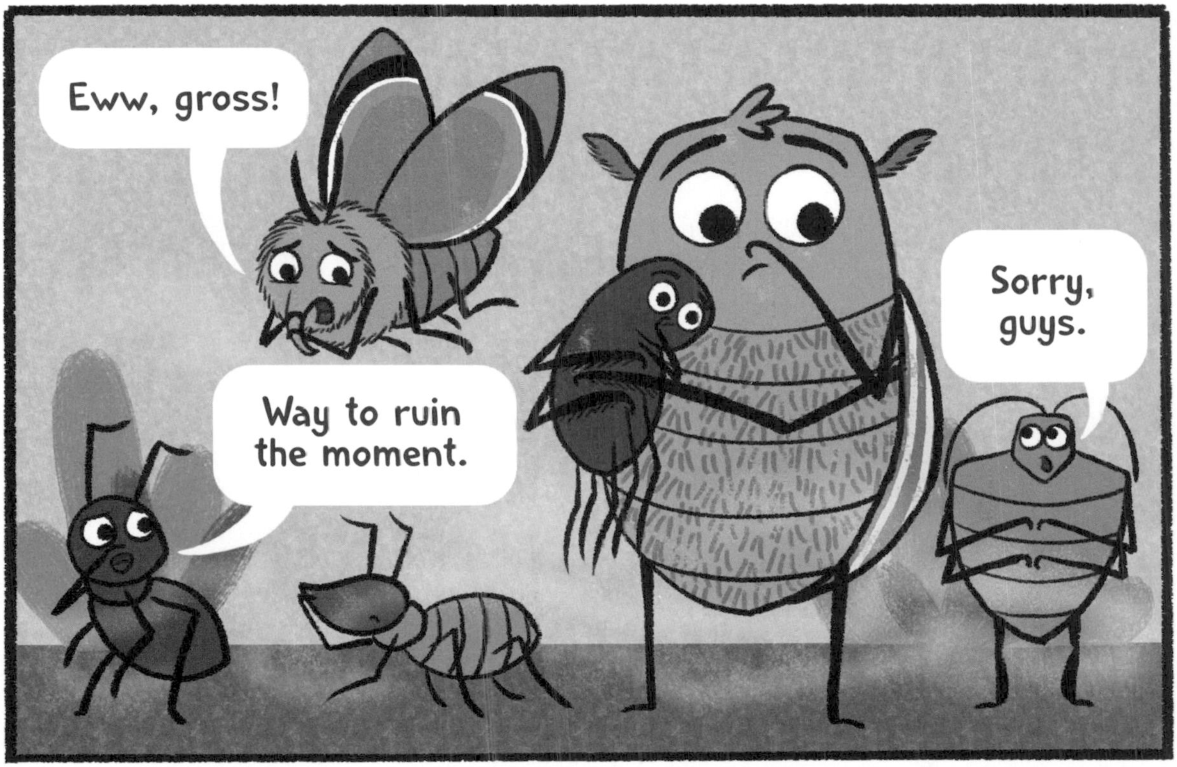
Eww, gross!
Way to ruin the moment.
Sorry, guys.

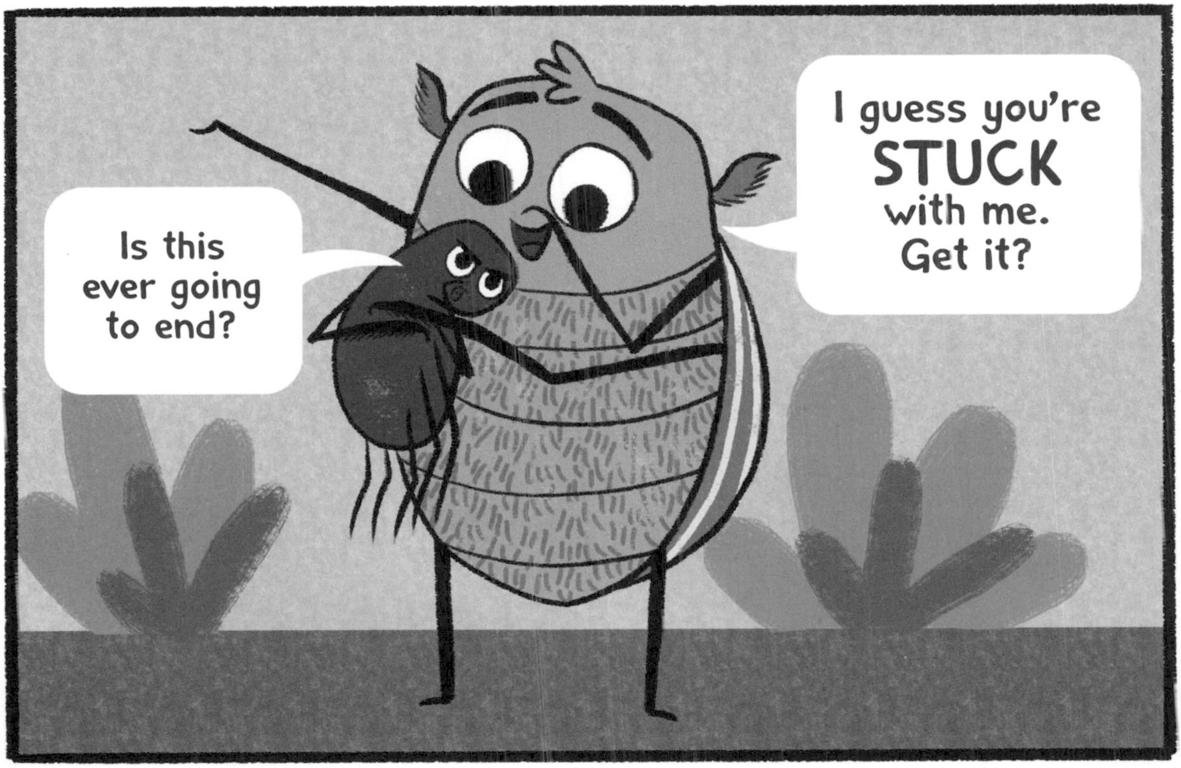
I guess you're STUCK with me. Get it?
Is this ever going to end?

AWESOME INSECT SUPER FACTS

Ants are strong, but the STRONGEST insect in the world is the horned dung beetle. It can pull 1141 times its weight. That's like dragging two semitrucks behind you.

But imagine the trucks are made of POOP!

The FASTEST flying insect is the dragonfly, flying up to 58 kilometers (36 miles) an hour! The Australian tiger beetle is the fastest land insect, running up to 9 kilometers (5.6 miles) an hour.

Race you?

You're on!

Hawk moths can make an ULTRASONIC sound that jams the echolocation ability of predators. (Ultrasonic sound is a sound that humans can't hear. Echolocation is the way some animals locate things by making sounds and listening for the echo.) That means hawk moths use noise to make themselves invisible to predators!

Now you see me, now you don't!

The nasute termite sprays a paralyzing toxin, making predators unable to move, but the bombardier beetle takes it up a notch by spraying BOILING HOT poison at its enemies!

Boiling hot bum poison, coming up!

I'm really glad I can't see that.

For Duncan — cousin, friend and puzzler extraordinaire

Published in Canada and the U.S. by Kids Can Press Ltd.
25 Dockside Drive, Toronto, ON M5A 0B5

Kids Can Press is a Corus Entertainment Inc. company

www.kidscanpress.com

The artwork in this book was rendered digitally with minimal leg flailing.
The text is set in Comical.

Edited by Yasemin Uçar.
Designed by Karen Powers.

Printed and bound in Shenzhen, China, in 10/2020 by C & C Offset

CM 21 0 9 8 7 6 5 4 3 2 1

FSC www.fsc.org MIX Paper from responsible sources FSC® C008047

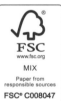

Library and Archives Canada Cataloguing in Publication

Title: Burt the Beetle doesn't bite / by Ashley Spires.
Other titles: Burt the Beetle does not bite
Names: Spires, Ashley, 1978– author, artist.
Description: Series statement: Burt the Beetle
Identifiers: Canadiana 20200317318 | ISBN 9781525301469 (hardcover)
Subjects: LCGFT: Graphic novels.
Classification: LCC PN6733.S66 B87 2021 | DDC j741.5/971 — dc23

Kids Can Press gratefully acknowledges that the land on which our office is located is the traditional territory of many nations, including the Mississaugas of the Credit, the Anishnabeg, the Chippewa, the Haudenosaunee and the Wendat peoples, and is now home to many diverse First Nations, Inuit and Métis peoples.

We thank the Government of Ontario, through Ontario Creates; the Ontario Arts Council; the Canada Council for the Arts; and the Government of Canada for supporting our publishing activity.